ROUGH COUNTRY

Cougar raised the boot gun and fired into the astonished features of Jake Schulster. The man's face disappeared into scarlet pulp, the back of his head erupting like a tiny volcano.

Before McClean could recover from the shock of the unexpected gunshot, Cougar hurled himself at the tall bounty hunter's legs. McClean cried out as his feet were bowled out from under him. He fell to all fours, but swiftly slashed the Bowie at his still-bound opponent. Cougar sat up and swung the now-empty Hopkins & Allen. The iron barrel smashed into the other bounty hunter's wrist, knocking the knife from numbed fingers.

McClean grunted, glared at his adversary, and then launched himself at Cougar, who drew his knees to his chest, allowing his opponent to close in. Then he launched both feet upward, driving the heels of his boots into McClean's face. The man's head snapped back, blood issuing from his smashed mouth. He slumped to the floor unconscious.

"Right now, you don't look so big, Mac," Cougar muttered.

Also by W.L. Fieldhouse:

KLAW
TOWN OF BLOOD
THE RATTLER GANG
GUN LUST

GUN LUST #2:

COMANCHERO KILL

W.L. Fieldhouse

LEISURE BOOKS ∞ NEW YORK CITY

Dedicated to Miss Debbie Slagle,

a very special lady.

A LEISURE BOOK

Published by

Dorchester Publishing Co., Inc.
41 E. 60 St.
New York City

Printed in the United States of America

ONE

Captain Bradly placed a gloved hand on the bulky multibarreled weapon. He appreciated a well-made gun and this was one of the best, most formidable instruments of warfare and destruction in the world. The captain smiled.

"Beautiful," he whispered meaningfully.

"They look a lot better than they work if'n you ask me, sir," Sergeant Lutz muttered. The grizzled, beefy NCO leaned his head to one side and spat a stream of brown juice out the open door of the boxcar.

"I don't recall asking you, Sergeant," Bradly remarked dryly. "But why do you condemn the Gatling gun?"

"The Johnny Rebs come up with this overgrown pepperbox, sir," Lutz replied, chewing his tobacco plug systematically. "When I was with General Sheridan durin' the war, we come up against these things once or twice. They jammed up half the time. Leave it to a Johnny Reb to make a fancy piece of junk and call it a weapon. No wonder we whupped 'em so easy."

"I remember the war too, Sergeant," the captain commented. "And I don't recall any time that 'whupping' the Confederates was easy. In fact, they probably won more battles than we did."

5

"But they didn't win the war." The noncom smiled, a trickle of brown fluid dribbling from the corner of his mouth to stain his brown-and gray-streaked beard.

"The Union did have a few advantages in the conflict, Sergeant," Bradly said. "Most of the industrialization was located in the northern states. We had more factories and thus we were better able to manufacture guns and cannons. There were also more men in our armies, although I wouldn't say they were any braver than the rebel troops. In fact, the Confederates generally seemed far more motivated to their cause."

"That's 'cause they wanted to keep their nigger slaves." Lutz shrugged.

"Most of those southern farmboys never even saw a black man, much less owned one." Bradly sighed. "No, the Confederates believed the federal government threatened their States' Rights. That's why they seceded from the Union—which, according to the Constitution, they had every right to do. However, Washington and President Lincoln didn't agree. So we wound up with four years of Civil War."

"And we won and that's what matters," Sergeant Lutz insisted.

"Many would agree with you, Sergeant," the captain admitted. "But I like to think we learned something of value from the War Between the States."

"What's that, sir?"

"How to prevent it from happening again," Bradly replied with a weak smile. "At any rate, Sergeant, your criticism of the original gun developed by Dr. Richard Gatling is valid. The early Gatlings *did* tend to jam and misfire under steady use. These models, however, have been modified and improved. Tests indicate the new Gatling guns are far more depèndable and require less maintenance than their Rebel forerunners."

"They don't look near as big to me as the ones we faced when the Confederates was shootin' at us."

"Part of that might be psychological," Bradly replied. "But these models are a smaller caliber. The original Gatlings were fifty to fifty-eight caliber, something that put considerable strain on the firing mechanism and might explain its tendency to misfire. The new Gatling is forty-four caliber, which makes it easier to handle and service."

"Well, I hope the Army likes its new toys," Lutz remarked cynically. He turned and spat another stream of tobacco out the door.

"What the hell!" a startled private exclaimed, backing away from the boxcar as he mopped the brown stain from his face with the palm of a hand.

"You should be more careful, Sergeant," Bradly commented. "And thankful you didn't hit an officer."

"Amen, sir," Lutz agreed.

The captain stepped to the edge of the doorway and gazed down at the detail of soldiers standing outside. Several men chuckled at their disgruntled companion who was still wiping tobacco juice from his face. They fell silent and came to attention when they saw the twin bars on the officer's uniform tunic.

"No cause for alarm, gentlemen," Bradly assured them. "Sergeant Lutz just had a little accident, but he's agreed to hold his fire and he's about out of ammunition anyway."

The men smiled in reply. Lutz snorted sourly.

"You six troopers know your mission," the captain continued. "You're to guard the seven Gatling guns on board this train. We'll be delivering three guns to Fort Clark, two to Fort Duncan, and the other two to Fort McCullen. Any questions?"

"We're goin' through a lot of Indian territory, ain't we, sir?" a young, soft-faced private asked.

"Most of Texas is still pretty much Indian territory, soldier," Bradly replied. "But the Comanches and Kiowas are mostly to the north of us and the few Apaches around here tend to be disorganized bands far too small to attack a train. Besides, Apaches don't like taking unnecessary chances, and the risks involved in tangling with a train full of troops is more than they'd be apt to figure the rewards would be worth."

"If redskins ain't a problem, how come we got so many men guardin' this train, sir?" another trooper inquired.

"Because we've got valuable cargo on board and we can't take any chances with it," the captain explained. "Besides, forty men isn't that many, although I'll admit this is a relatively small train. Any other questions?"

There were none.

"Very well, men." Bradly nodded. "Climb aboard and let's hope we all enjoy the ride without any incidents."

"Amen to that, sir," Sergeant Lutz remarked sincerely.

The train moved at a steady pace, neither rushing nor crawling along the tracks. It traveled several hundred miles through dry prairies and occasional grassy plains. At night, Captain Bradly posted additional sentries on the cars, realizing the belief that Indians won't attack after sundown to be as unreliable as a politician's campaign promises. But the journey remained uneventful . . .

Until the following afternoon.

Passing through a forest, the engineer slowed the train slightly to take advantage of the rare, but welcome, shade provided by the natural ceiling of leafy branches that extended above the locomotive. Occasionally the roofs of the boxcars would strike a low hanging limb. The troops soon ignored the *thump-thump* sound from the ceilings. Thus they failed to notice when several booted feet landed on the roofs.

Unaware that uninvited passengers had dropped down from the trees and now rode topside, the Army train kept going. It soon climbed a slightly inclined hill in an otherwise flat prairie. Rock formations flanked both sides of the tracks, giant gray and red monuments carved into bizarre sculptures by millions of years exposure to the elements.

"Holy shit!" Harv Jenson, the engineer, exclaimed. His eyes widened with surprise and fear when he saw a pile of boulders sitting in the center of the tracks at the top of the hill. "Brace yourself," he warned his assistant as he grabbed the brake.

The train screeched to a desperate halt, its momentum still carrying it into the barrier. Metal collided harshly with stone, creating an ugly sound but

9

little damage.

"Fuckin' rockslide," Tim Kenner, the co-engineer growled.

"Like hell," Jenson replied sharply. "There ain't no rocks around them tracks, just them big bastards smack dab in the middle. Go back and tell them soldier boys to get off their butts and get ready for trouble!"

"Jesus . . ." the assistant gasped, realizing the implications of the engineer's statement.

"No, *señor,*" a deep baritone voice announced.

They turned to see a huge figure at the coal bins. Clad in a filthy gray shirt, which may have once been white, and baggy trousers, the man stood six foot four with enormous shoulders and a chest that resembled a beer keg. Dense black hair covered most of his head and face, but his small dark eyes and wide flat nose were plainly visible. A wide smile revealed surprisingly white teeth as he raised a shovel in one large hand.

"Not Jesus," he explained, jabbing a thumb to his buffalo chest. "Luis!"

Then he swung the shovel in a fast cross-body stroke, slamming the blade into Tim Kenner's face. Bone crunched as the blow propelled the man backward. Kenner fell into the gears of the engine, blood spurting from his nose and mouth. Then he slumped to the coal-dust-strewn floor.

Harv Jenson lunged for a Spencer repeater he kept in a corner in case of outlaws or hostile Indians. He never reached the carbine. Luis brought the shovel down hard on the engineer's skull. Jenson collapsed with a groan. The giant Mexican laughed and raised the tool for another blow.

"Why have we stopped?" Captain Bradly demanded as he entered a passenger car full of soldiers commanded by Lieutenant Fine.

"I don't know, sir," the young officer nervously replied. His acne-scarred face revealed his distress.

"Find out and position your men at their assigned areas by the windows in case we've got a *real* problem on our hands."

"Yes, Captain." The lieutenant saluted briskly.

Bradly left the passenger car and moved across the narrow platform to the next compartment. A shadow suddenly fell upon him like a humanoid eclipse. Alarmed, he looked up and clawed at the flap holster on his hip.

A long slither of light flashed from an obscure shape on the roof of the car. Sharp steel struck the side of Captain Bradly's neck, severing carotid artery and jugular in one brutal stroke. Blood spewed from the ghastly wound as the officer vainly tried to clear his .44 Army Colt from its holster. His mouth opend to cry out, but crimson bubbled from his lips instead of words. Captain Martin Bradly toppled to the ground in a twitching, dying heap.

Ramon Larson wiped a rag along the blade of his cutlass and slid the short sword into a bright red sash around his narrow waist. His dark, handsome features expressed satisfaction with his work. Larson did not find sadistic pleasure in killing, but it was part of his business and he regarded it as a necessary step to making a profit.

11

Nimbly, the slender *mestizo* swung down from the roof to the platform of the car and opened the door. Inside, five Comancheros held Sergeant Lutz, two privates, and a corporal at gun point. They wore an assortment of dusty *vaquero* clothing and denim with bandoliers crisscrossing their chests. Larson's followers were as vicious and cruel as their appearance suggested.

Dirty and unshaven, the Comancheros glared at their prisoners coldly. Three of them were former *bandidos,* another had been an outlaw in Missouri, and the fifth was a renegade half-breed Yaqui-Mexican. Ramon Larson smiled at the group.

"I trust our *gringo* friends are not too comfortable?" he inquired.

"We tied their hands behind their backs like you told us, Ramon," Arlon Ford declared. Wanted for bank robbery, rape, and murder, the overweight, dough-faced outlaw might have resembled a whiskey drummer if he'd used a razor, soap and water and dressed accordingly.

"Then we can talk, eh?" Ramon remarked as he approached the soldiers. "I just met your *capitan* outside, but he was rude and did not introduce himself. I would like to know his name."

"You murderin' bastard . . ." Lutz snarled, but one of the Mexican Comancheros rammed a rifle butt into his stomach. The sergeant's sentence ended in a choking gasp.

"Ah, my friend," Larson mused, drawing his cutlass slowly. "You wish to prove your courage, no?" He placed the tip of the sword under the NCO's bearded chin. "What is the *capitan's* name, brave one?"

Lutz inhaled deeply, regaining his breath. He glared defiantly up at the Comanchero leader. "Go to hell, you greaser shit!"

Ramon shoved the blade into the hollow of Sergeant Lutz's throat. The noncom's mouth opened to form a mute oval. Blood and half-chewed tobacco spilled onto his beard. Larson jerked his cutlass free and the sergeant wilted to the floor and died.

"Now, I ask you the same question," he declared, pointing the red-stained sword at one of the enlisted men.

"Captain Bradly," the soldier replied quickly.

"Gracias," Larson bowed politely. "I appreciate your cooperation."

Then he drove the cutlass through the trooper's heart. The Yaqui half-breed, who'd adopted the simple name, Miguel, when he'd joined the Comancheros, quickly slit the throat of the other private with a bone-handled Bowie knife. Before the corporal could utter a sound, a Mexican Comanchero clamped a dirty palm over his mouth and rammed the slender blade of a dirk between his ribs.

"Bueno!" Larson declared, fastidiously wiping the cutlass clean before returning it to his sash.

Lieutenant Fine, escorted by two armed troops, climbed down from the train and headed toward the engine. The long barrel of a Spencer suddenly swung around the edge of the engine. Fine stared into the gaping muzzle of the big rifle an instant before it roared, blasting a .52 caliber bullet into the center of

13

the officer's face.

The two startled enlisted men swung their carbines toward the concealed sniper. Something sliced through the air above them and cracked sharply like a small caliber pistol. A tough cord of leather snaked around the barrel of one of the trooper's weapons, yanking it from his grasp. Both soldiers turned to see a lanky, rawboned figure clad in patched overalls and a shapeless ten-gallon hat, atop the roof of the nearest boxcar. His teeth grimaced amid a long, unkempt red beard as he drew back the bullwhip in his right hand and cocked a .36 caliber Navy Colt in his left. The revolver discharged a lead ball, ripping a destructive path through the side of the armed private's neck. Gore spewed from the ragged exit wound and the soldier stumbled and fell.

Weaponless, the surviving trooper glanced helplessly from the muzzle of the Spencer to the pistolman on the roof. He tried to dive for the discarded carbine, but Luis fired the Spencer once more. A heavy slug smashed into the private's ribcage, throwing his bleeding body five feet to collide against the side of a boxcar.

"Yeee-aa!" Jethro Mackall, the Ozark hillbilly turned Comanchero whooped. "How do yee like this chile's brand o' medicine, yee blue-bellied bas-turds?"

The shots spurred the troops within the train into action. They bolted to their prearranged positions at the windows, cocking weapons and shattering glass with gun barrels. Two dozen Comacheros, however, were already in position among the rock formations surrounding the train. A volley of rifle fire exploded from the boulders. A soldier took a bullet through the forehead and fell dead. Another private's jawbone was blown off and a third suffered a broken collarbone from an enemy rifle slug.

Ramon Larson and five Comancheros moved cautiously along the length of the train until they joined Wesley Quint at the compartment containing the Gatling guns. Quint had earned an infamous reputation as one of the deadliest pistolmen in the southwestern United States. He was short and lean muscled, and his stern face resembled an axe blade with eyeballs. Within less than a year, he had risen to second in command in the Comanchero gang. Since Ramon Larson had little admiration for the Yankees, this was no small accomplishment.

Larson whispered two curt words to the pistolman. Quint nodded in reply and drew a Smith & Wesson revolver from the low hung holster on his hip. He hammered a gloved fist on the boxcar and cocked the gun.

"This is Captain Bradly!" he shouted. "We're under siege! Open up!"

The door of the compartment slid open and a frightened trooper gazed down at Quint. The Smith & Wesson snarled. A .44 slug tore a merciless path through the bridge of the soldier's nose into his brain.

Quint sprang through the entrance of the boxcar like a panther, dropping to one knee and quickly training his weapon on another startled trooper. Before the young private could react to the unexpected threat, the hammer of the Smith & Wesson fell and a bullet smashed into his heart.

15

Larson shoved the door to widen the entrance for the rest of his men. Quint swung the muzzle of his smoking revolver toward two terrified soldiers. His free hand fanned the hammer, blasting three rapid rounds into the uniformed chests of his victims. Larson fired a silver-plated Remington and gut-shot another private. A Comanchero thrust the twin barrels of a ten gauge Parker shotgun into the boxcar and squeezed a trigger. The last member of the detail received a lethal dose of buckshot that pulverized his chest and destroyed his heart and lungs.

Deadly lead hail continued to hiss fiercely from all directions. Although the Comancheros' shots effectively pinned down the soldiers in the train, a handful of the defenders' rounds claimed hits among the ambushers. Rifle slugs sent three wounded Comancheros tumbling from their hiding places among the rocks.

A young buck sergeant boldly (if foolishly) stepped onto the platform of a passenger car and leveled his Colt on the group by the Gatling gun car. Two of his pistol shots struck the broad back of a fat Mexican outlaw and a third punctured Arlon Ford's right triceps muscle. The portly badman screamed, half spun and fell to his knees, clutching his bloodied upper arm. However, the sergeant then paid for his moment of glory as a volley of sniper bullets pelted his upper torso and hurled his ravaged body over the handrail of the platform.

Ramon Larson hardly noticed when his men fell in battle. They all knew the dangers involved in the Comanchero trade and they accepted the risks in

16

hopes of satisfying their own lusts for profit and bloodshed. The ringleader's primary concern was self-preservation and the Gatling guns—in that order. To his relief, he saw Luis and Jethro Mackall had slithered from the front of the train to the boxcar containing the prized mutlibarreled weapons. The giant Mexican uncoupled the links of the compartment from the car in front of it.

"Now!" Ramon ordered, waving his cutlass dramatically. *"Vamanos!"*

The last four train cars, including the one with the guns, began to roll backward down the hill. Larson quickly climbed aboard. Other Comancheros followed his example. Most of the gang amid the rocks still fired enough rounds to keep the soldiers at bay while others descended the opposite side to get horses ready for a hasty retreat.

The four disjointed train cars rattled past the foot of the hill. They rolled almost two miles on their own momentum and might have traveled twice as far if some of Larson's accomplices had not already been assigned to disconnect the track rails. The caboose and the box cars came to an abrupt, but not destructive halt.

Ramon Larson and his Comancheros then loaded the Gatling guns onto two large Conestoga wagons. By the time they were ready to transport the weapons in the vehicles, the members of the outlaw gang who'd been stationed at the boulders for the ambush galloped into view.

"How many men did we lose?" Larson asked sharply. He didn't really care, but he knew he had to express some concern for his Comancheros or he wouldn't be able to command *or* trust them.

"We had to leave five men behind," Juan Alverez, a former *bandido* in charge of the sniper detail replied gravely. "Two are dead for certain. The others are wounded, probably dying."

"For their loss I grieve," the Comanchero leader said, displaying an expression of profound sorrow for men he didn't give a shit about. "At least we have the Gatling guns, so they didn't die in vain," he added. "Those guns mean we'll have power, wealth, and invincibility."

"What's int-vince. . ." Jethro Mackall asked lamely. "That word mean? Is it like nobody can see you?"

"It's better than that." Ramon Larson smiled coldly. "It means nobody can stop us and I dare anyone to try!"

TWO

"I'm telling you it's all there in the manual," Alexander Shaddrock insisted, turning in his saddle to glare at his partner.

"Yeah," Thomas Cruthers, the legendary Cougar, muttered as he tugged the wide brim of his Montana peaked hat to shield his eyes from the glare of the Texas sun. "They also got books that tell about flying horses, nine-headed monsters, and women with snakes for hair. Reckon you believe that's true too."

"It was written by one of the greatest pugilists in England," Shaddrock continued, irritated by his companion's attitude. "He proves that a man who knows the principles of boxing can defend himself by using only his fists."

Cougar chuckled. A smile seemed alien on his generally impassive face. "I bet you won't be able to punch a bullet no matter how many books you read."

"Aw, shit," the other man snorted. "I'm not talking about weapons. I mean when you've got to fight some big bastard with just your bare knuckles."

"Seems I recall having such encounters from time to time." Cougar yawned. Forty-three years old, he'd been hunting men for more than two decades. Cougar still wore his gray tunic with a major's oakleaves on the shoulders. He often described his time in the Confederate Army as "four years of a different kind of bounty hunting."

Shaddrock felt a trifle foolish lecturing the senior man in fighting. His partner could kill with his bare hands and had done so more than once. Still, the younger regulator continued. "Well, all that kicking, butting, and grappling isn't necessary if you know the science of pugilism."

"Science, huh?" Cougar grinned, raising the corners of the drooping black mustache that accented the frown he usually wore.

"It consists of timing, moving your body to avoid the other man's punches," Shaddrock explained. "Then knowing how to throw the most effective blows—left jab, left hook, right cross, and uppercut."

"Hell, Shaddrock." The older man sighed. "You've done pretty well with the rough 'n' tumble style of fighting you picked up in the street brawls back east and when you and the other Yankee soldiers used to fight over who'd lead when you danced at the military balls."

"V-ery funny," Shaddrock growled. He'd served as a first lieutenant in the Union infantry. "I heard some pretty naughty stories about why you Arkansas boys keep sheep in your house too."

"My point is, you shouldn't replace what you already know with this science of pugilism crap." Cougar shrugged.

"You fight your way, I'll fight mine," Shaddrock said sharply. "Next you'll be trying to tell me what kind of weapons to carry."

"Maybe you better study up on this boxing after all," Cougar remarked. "Since you use such pea-shooters, a feller might keep coming after you shot him and punch you in the nose."

Shaddrock's firearms were actually more formidable than his partner's barb suggested. The younger bounty hunter carried a matched pair of .36 caliber Police Colts in a shoulder holster rig. The walnut grips of the cap and ball revolvers jutted from under Shaddrock's arms, as he'd removed his suit jacket while riding in the afternoon heat. The stock of a brass framed Henry repeater extended from a boot on his saddle. The Easterner often carried a small hide-out gun and a set of brass knuckle-dusters.

Cougar's choice of weapons consisted of larger caliber guns. At his right, a twelve gauge Greener shotgun with sawed-off barrels rode in a saddle boot. On the left was a .56 Sharps muzzle loader, an accurate and deadly rifle in the hands of a marksman like Thomas Cruthers. A big .44 Colt Dragoon filled a holster on his right hip. When Cougar shot a man, he used something that would bring him down with one round and keep him down until the undertaker arrived. He also wore a large combat Bowie on his belt. The sheath was positioned for a cross-draw. A thong draped the quillion to hold the knife in place, but a simple brush of thumb or finger would unfasten the leather and allow the Bowie to be brought into action immediately.

Their physical appearance differed as much as their taste in firearms. Shaddrock was six foot two, lean muscled and strikingly handsome with Nordic features, blue eyes, and blond hair. Cougar stood four inches shorter than his partner, although he was the more muscular of the pair. His craggy Slavic face had been deeply lined by exposure to the elements and many years of hard experience. Some considered Cougar ugly, others found him compelling and attractive, but no one ignored him.

The bounty hunters were very different individuals in many ways, but they'd formed a close friendship and a partnership that made them the most efficient and formidable team of man stalkers in the West.

As they rode into Rio Polvo, Shaddrock scanned over the town. The only items that made it different from a hundred other small communities was the fact the hotel and saloon were larger than most—no doubt to accommodate uniformed patrons from Fort Mc-Cullen less than two miles away.

"Bet that hotel does double duty as a whorehouse," Shaddrock mused hopefully.

"Don't you ever think of anything else?" Cougar muttered. "I know you young fellas got some wild oats to sow, but you're the most seed-throwin' son of a bitch I ever met."

"A man does what he's good at." Shaddrock shrugged. "But right now I'm also wondering why the Army wants to hire us. Since when has the military had to pay civilians to do their job for them?"

"Hell, the Army has always hired civilians—scouts, mule skinners, sometimes advisors and instructors."

"Don't tell me they want us to teach the troops how to hunt down wanted men." Shaddrock snorted. "There's enough competition in this business."

22

"There are certain things a bounty hunter can do a lawman can't," Cougar remarked. "Reckon there's times one can do things a whole Army can't as well."

"Such as?"

"Shaddrock, you know as much about this as I do." The senior man sighed. "You were right there with me in Amarillo when that fancy warrant officer walked up to us and asked if we'd be interested in a twenty thousand dollar reward."

"Which is sort'a like asking a couple town drunks if they'd like to have limitless credit at the local saloon," his partner commented.

"Then he gave us each a thousand dollars and told us to be at Fort McCullen on the fourteenth," Cougar concluded.

"Sure hope he wasn't a recruiter." Shaddrock snorted. "I'd just as soon we hadn't arrived a day early either."

"How's that?"

"Tomorrow is a Saturday."

"You suddenly decide not to work on weekends or something?"

"This is Friday the thirteenth," the younger hunter said ominously.

"Oh, hell." Cougar groaned.

"It's an unlucky day by tradition and there must be a reason for it."

"So other fellers can get a laugh out of superstitious jackasses like you," the senior man replied. "Personally, I never feel very lucky, but I do get thirsty from time to time."

Shaddrock smiled. "Yeah, that saloon looks mighty

good to me too."

"Good." Cougar nodded. "Then you're buying the beers."

Shaddrock cursed under his breath.

The bounty hunters tied their horses to the hitching rail and entered the saloon. It resembled numerous other taverns they'd visited in the Southwest. The bar was longer and better than most, constructed of solid maple with well-stocked shelves of whiskey and tequila behind it. A thin, bald bartender stood at his station, his weary expression suggesting he spent more time sucking lemons than sampling his products.

Smoke rose from occupied tables. A portly man in a white shirt and vest played solitaire and sipped redeye as he examined the cards with a bored sigh. A group of soldiers played five card stud for matchsticks and shared a pitcher of beer. Three privates faked interest as a burly sergeant shuffled the cards and bragged about his combat experience.

Brass cuspidors were positioned by the tables and bar, yet the patrons seemed to ignore them, spitting carelessly on the sawdust-covered floor. To Shaddrock's dismay, there were no women present.

The pair strolled to the bar. Cougar placed his short-barreled Greener on the counter while Shaddrock ordered the drinks. "Two beers," he told the bartender. "Cheapest you've got."

"Only have one kind," the sour-faced man behind the bar answered. "You figure this is some fancy place in San Francisco, feller?"

"This wouldn't qualify as a fancy place in a Philadelphia slum district," Shaddrock stated. "Just try to find a couple clean mugs and fill them with something that doesn't taste like mule piss."

The bartender muttered unintelligibly as he turned to rinse two glass mugs in a basin of greasy water.

"You got a thousand bucks in your pocket and you still act like a skinflint." Cougar shook his head. "Beats me how you Yankees won the war. I'm surprised you were willing to pay for the bullets."

"What is this shit?" Shaddrock snapped. "You're the biggest miser I know. If you're such a high roller, you buy the beers."

"You already done it." Cougar shrugged.

"Not yet." The younger man grinned.

The bartender put two foam-covered mugs on the counter. "Ten cents," he announced.

"Well," Shaddrock glared at his partner.

"It's your turn."

"You can have it."

"I wouldn't want to embarrass you in public."

"Since when? Pay up or shut up."

"Just give ol' Pete a nickel, dude," the sergeant declared as he walked purposefully to the bar, closely followed by the other soldiers. " 'Cause that's all yore gonna need."

"You fellers ain't offering to buy one of us a drink, are you?" Cougar inquired.

"You just haul yore ass outta this saloon," Sergeant Frank Cooper snarled, folding his thick arms akimbo on his muscular chest. "No half-breed is welcome in a white man's saloon—especially a goddamn Johnny Reb like you."

25

"What's your problem, fella?" Shaddrock snapped back at the NCO. "The war's been over for quite a while and you don't own this saloon so it's none of your business who comes in here."

"You got a goddamn southern white trash bastard with Injun blood in his veins for a friend," Cooper hissed. The troops behind him slowly formed a semicircle around the bounty hunters.

"To be honest," Cougar began, raising his mug to his lips. "I ain't sure if I'm part Indian or Mexican myself—and I don't really give a damn."

Without warning, he swung the glass, dashing the contents into the faces of Cooper and an enlisted man named Brown. Another trooper rushed forward and tried to grab the bounty hunter. Cougar cracked the heavy glass against the man's jaw. The ambitious Private Wells staggered along the length of the bar before he slumped to the floor in a dazed heap.

Private Hatcher jumped back, alarm written on his youthful features. Cougar hurled the mug at him. The trooper quickly ducked, only to receive a deerskin boot in the face when the bounty hunter stepped in and delivered a well-aimed kick. Hatcher sprawled across the saloon and lay still.

Sergeant Cooper and Private Brown cursed as they mopped beer from their eyes before rejoining the battle. Suddenly, Shaddrock moved into their way, his fists held at eye level. The soldiers stared at him, surprised by his boxing stance.

"Come on, fat boy," Shaddrock taunted, watching the big NCO between his balled hands. "Prepare to defend . . ."

The bounty hunter then realized he'd raised his arms too high and lowered them, trying to emulate the pugilist positions he'd seen in his manual. Frank Cooper's big fist shot between Shaddrock's parted hands and crashed into his jaw. The blow sent the regulator reeling across the room.

Private Brown attacked Cougar, apparently unimpressed by the fact his two comrades had already been rendered unconscious by the senior bounty hunter. A tall lanky ex-farmboy, the trooper charged, throwing wild, roundhouse swings with his long arms. Cougar did the unexpected—he stepped forward and seized the soldier's sleeves. Before the startled Brown could react, the regulator butted his forehead into the man's nose.

Cougar released the dazed man and smashed a fist into his face, knocking the trooper into a wall near the fat solitaire player. Private Brown slid to the floor as the half-drunk loner bolted from his chair, abandoning his table.

Sergeant Cooper tried to wrap his burly arms around Cougar from behind. Before he could apply the bone-crushing "bear hug," the bounty hunter drove an elbow into his breastbone. Cooper gasped and staggered four feet. With a snarl, he prepared to launch another attack, but Shaddrock appeared in front of him once more.

The younger bounty hunter jabbed his left fist into the point of Cooper's jaw—once, twice, three times. The noncom's head snapped back from the fast smooth punches. Shaddrock then hurled a right cross at his opponent's battered chin. He missed. Cooper

27

had stepped to one side. The bounty hunter had put all his weight into the last punch and his forward momentum threw him off balance long enough to allow the sergeant to grab a chair. He smashed it across Shaddrock's back. Fortunately for the regulator, the chair had been damaged before and mended with chicken wire. Thus, two wooden legs shattered instead of Shaddrock's spine.

"Some folks just don't have no respect for science," Cougar called out.

"Shut up," Shaddrock rasped, again assuming a boxing stance as Sergeant Cooper discarded the bulk of the chair and gathered up one of the broken legs.

"I'm gonna bust yore head, boy!" he declared, wielding the improvised club.

"Oh, fuck it!" Shaddrock exclaimed.

Cooper charged forward. The bounty hunter's leg suddenly flashed and he kicked the big man between the legs. The NCO's mouth formed a black oval as he dropped the chair leg and clawed at his agonized genitals. Shaddrock seized one of the sergeant's arms and hurled him savagely into the bar. Cooper groaned when the small of his back connected with the counter.

"You just had to do it, didn't you?" the bounty hunter complained. He clasped his hands together and swung a brutal chop to Cooper's midsection. The noncom doubled up with a moan.

"You had to prove my book and the science of pugilism were wrong," Shaddrock continued. He folded a knee and whipped it into Cooper's face hard. "What's worse," the regulator declared, catching the soldier

28

by the front of his tunic. "You just had to prove Cougar was *right!*"

He glared at the unconscious, bloodstained face of Frank Cooper and shoved the man aside, allowing him to fall heavily to the floor. Cougar approached the bar.

"Don't say anything," Shaddrock growled.

"I ain't gonna say I told you so," Cougar replied mildly. "Where's the bartender?"

"I guess he left." The other bounty hunter shrugged.

"Hell, I sort'a spilled my beer," Cougar said. "Figured you might buy me another one."

"Why don't you . . ."

Shaddrock's remark ended abruptly as he saw Private Brown had recovered enough energy to again present a threat. The soldier seized a bottle of redeye left by the card player and charged, swinging it at Cougar's head.

The senior bounty hunter also saw Brown's attack and nimbly dodged the bottle. Shaddrock grabbed the soldier's wrist. Cougar's hands caught Brown's other arm and belt. Together, they picked up the trooper and hurled him over the bar. Brown screamed briefly before he crashed to the floor behind the counter.

"You can get us a couple beers while you're back there," Cougar muttered.

"*You're* buying," Shaddrock told him.

The other regulator shrugged.

"That's them, Sheriff!" the pinch-faced bartender announced as he and a tall, broad-shouldered figure with a copper badge on his shirt appeared at the batwings. The lawman held a revolver in his fist.

"You boys are under arrest," he drawled slowly, his thumb oarring back the hammer of his gun.

"Hold on a minute, Sheriff," Cougar urged. "These soldiers started the fight. Hell, there's four of them and two of us. You figure we'd be stupid enough to go against those odds if we didn't have to?"

"Don't rightly know how stupid you are, Major," Sheriff Fred Curtis declared. "The Army handles its own troublemakers and I take care of the civilians. Ya'll wearin' a Confederate tunic, but the war's over and our side lost. So come along peaceful, Major. I don't wanta have to shoot a fellow Southerner."

"Listen, Sheriff," Shaddrock began. "We've got an appointment to see Colonel Sutton at Fort McCullen . . ."

"Ya'll got an appointment at a jail cell, son," Curtis replied grimly. "I'm gettin' a might weary o' tellin' you two to come along too."

The batwings parted and a young second lieutenant entered. "Oh!" he exclaimed. "Excuse me."

"Wait up, Lieutenant Barr," Curtis said. "You'd better get the provost and see about these troopers of your's who done got in a fight here."

"Oh, my," the young officer replied with embarrassment. "I'm afraid Sergeant Cooper and his men *are* the provost guard."

"Lieutenant," Shaddrock said. "Your commanding officer is expecting us at the fort tomorrow."

"He is?" Barr stared at the bounty hunters with surprise.

30

"Alexander Shaddrock and Cougar—Thomas Cruthers."

"Maybe you'll be goin' to the fort tomorrow," Sheriff Curtis remarked. "But you're spendin' tonight in jail. Now move!"

"Friday the thirteenth," Shaddrock muttered.

"Aw, hell," Cougar groaned.

THREE

Colonel Hathaway Sutton was a stout bullike man with a great cowhorn mustache and a shiny bald pate adorned by a mere fringe of white hair. He paced the artillery-red carpet of his office with his hands folded at the small of his back as he addressed his visitors.

"I don't mind telling you men that you haven't made an overwhelmingly good impression on me since I had to get you out of the town jail to have this conversation," the colonel announced gruffly.

"You'll have to have a talk with your provost patrol about that," Shaddrock replied, leaning back in an armchair and admiring the decor. Sutton's desk appeared to be genuine oak and the other furniture consisted of solid walnut and leather.

An oil painting of President Grant dominated one wall, but detailed maps ruled the others. A three-dimensional chart of southwest Texas and Mexico featured multicolored flags to represent Fort McCullen and other military bases (Mexican as well as American), locales of current Indian uprisings, and detachments of troops—past, present, and probable future. There was also a well-stocked liquor cabinet in one corner. Cougar helped himself to some French cognac.

"Colonel," the senior bounty hunter began. "The Army didn't pay us one thousand dollars each to come here and listen to a lecture about barroom brawls. If you were lookin' for a couple fellers with halos you should have sent a messenger to heaven."

Sutton glared at Cougar and said, "Actually, I don't approve of the plan. It was General Andrews' notion, not mine."

"But you have to follow orders, right, Colonel?" Shaddrock smiled. "So why don't you just tell us what we're supposed to do?"

"Last week, a train transporting seven Gatling guns—very efficient, modified versions of the original design—was ambushed by a large body of highly skilled and well-organized outlaws," Sutton explained. "More than half of the forty-man detail in charge of the guns were killed. The Gatlings were stolen."

"That doesn't sound like any nickel and dime gang," Cougar mused, raising a balloon-shaped glass to his lips. "Most wouldn't have much use for a weapon as big as a Gatling. Maybe some *Federales* crossed the border to get themselves some extra equipment for the Mexican Army. Wouldn't be the first time."

"We know who did it, Major Cruthers," Sutton replied. "Comancheros."

"Sounds like that must be extraordinary-cheros to pull off a job like that." Shaddrock chuckled.

The colonel frowned.

"You have to excuse my partner," Cougar stated, sipping his cognac. "He got shot in the head a while

33

back and it warped his sense of humor."

"The Comancheros are marauding bands of criminals," Sutton explained, his voice adopting the tone of a lecturer. "They are comprised of human scum of all types—Mexican bandits, American outlaws, Indian renegades, and other outcasts. They generally raid small farms and hamlets, stealing, raping, and killing like rabid dogs."

"I didn't know rabid dogs robbed and raped anything." Shaddrock said. "But go on with your story, Colonel."

Sutton's face reddened. "Other Comancheros, however, have discovered another way to make a lucrative, if illegal and immoral, profit—selling arms and liquor to Indians on either side of the border."

"Yaquis and Apaches are nomads," Cougar commented, taking a cigar from his pocket. "Can't see them hauling a Gatling around. Comanches or Kiowas might be interested in something like that to defend their tribes if another war with the pony soldiers breaks out."

"No wonder the Army is worried," Shaddrock added, rising from his chair to walk to the liquor cabinet.

"Seems to me the Texas Rangers generally handle the Comancheros," Cougar said, lighting his stogie. "They seem to do a pretty good job. If the Army can't do its own dirty work, why not call in the Rangers?"

Sutton clucked his tongue with disgust. "If you two aren't willing to accept this mission. . ."

"Hold on, Colonel," Shaddrock interrupted, gesturing with a bottle of cognac in his hand. "We aren't

34

in the Army and we aren't dumb-ass volunteers. We're bounty hunters. We track down men for a profit, but suicide missions aren't part of our profession."

"A bounty is exactly what you're being offered," the colonel assured him. "Twenty thousand dollars for the return of those Gatling guns and the man who stole them—Ramon Larson—dead or alive," Sutton added grimly. "Preferably dead."

"Larson, eh?" Cougar muttered. "Yeah, he's a bad one."

"You're familiar with the man, Major?"

"Just call me Cougar," the bounty hunter told him. "Everybody else does, even my enemies. I know Larson is supposed to be a shrewd son of a bitch who's been active along the border for the last couple years. Hear he fancies himself as a swashbuckler and carries a pirate sword. Not much of a weapon, but it works well enough on unsuspecting or helpless victims. He put together a gang of about fifty of the meanest bastards that ever cut their mothers' throats and they've been cutting a lot more ever since."

"Fifty men?" Shaddrock raised his eyebrows. "That does it!" He put the bottle back in the cabinet. "Let's get out of here."

"Afraid, Mr. Shaddrock?" Sutton asked softly.

"I'm not crazy, Colonel," the bounty hunter replied sharply. "Cougar and I are the best in the business, but two men against fifty..."

"Wait a minute," the senior regulator urged. "Let's hear the whole story before we leave."

"Jesus, Cougar." Shaddrock stared at his partner.

"I thought *you* were always telling *me* not to take foolish chances."

"Twenty thousand dollars is worth listening to, ain't it?" Cougar commented. "All right, Colonel. I'd appreciate an answer to my question now. Why isn't the Army or the Rangers handling Larson?"

"It's very simple," Sutton told him. "The Comancheros are headquartered in Mexico."

"That figures." Cougar nodded. "I've heard he's been selling weapons to *bandidos* and ragtag revolutionaries south of the border."

"Of course, this puts him outside the legal jurisdictions of both the United States cavalry and the Texas Rangers," Sutton concluded.

"But *we* can cross the border," Shaddrock stated. "Then you expect us to kidnap or kill Larson—which *isn't* legal and could get us thrown into a Mexican prison—and just roll seven Gatling guns back into the United States?"

"Something like that," Sutton admitted.

"And what do you figure those fifty Comancheros are going to be doing?" Shaddrock snarled. "Do we pour prune juice into their tequila and hope they'll be too busy shitting to notice we're stealing their fucking Gatling guns?"

"Actually, how you do it is your problem." Sutton shrugged. "According to our files, you two are supposed to be remarkably resourceful and clever. Improvise."

"Improvise, hell!" Shaddrock snapped. "The odds are too great. Get yourself somebody else to die for you, Colonel."

"I understand that you faced rather formidable odds in the past," Sutton declared. "And I doubt if the reward offered was greater than twenty thousand dollars."

"We weren't facing fifty guns either," Shaddrock answered.

"Additional money means additional risk in our business, Shaddrock," Cougar remarked thoughtfully.

"But a million dollar reward isn't worth a cow turd if you're dead!"

"There might be a way to handle this and live to collect the bounty," Cougar mused. "You seem to be mighty sure Larson had those Gatlings, Colonel. What's your source?"

"Not all of the Comancheros escaped unscathed," Sutton explained. "Our soldiers killed three of the raiders and two others were wounded. One died later, but the survivor is currently residing in our stockade. He's a minor lowlife named Arlon Ford. He was carrying some of his own wanted posters inside his shirt. The animal must be proud of his criminal activities."

"A lot of outlaws like to collect their own posters," Cougar said. "When they sit around the campfire with their own kind they can pull out one and say, 'Look what I did!' "

"Maybe we ought to open a printing press and sell phony posters to smalltime hootowls," Shaddrock suggested. "I bet a chicken thief would pay ten bucks to have 'proof' that he robbed a bank or shot it out with the sheriff's posse."

"Let's handle one job at a time," Cougar replied.

"All right. This Ford feller is our only real connection to Larson so we'll have to use him to lead us to the gang."

"If you're thinking of beating a confession from the man, I must remind you that Ford is a prisoner of a United States military installation," Sutton stated stiffly. "That means he's under our protection according to the Constitution which prohibits cruel or unusual punishments—such as skinning him alive with that Bowie knife of yours."

"If you've read up on us, you ought to know torture ain't one of our methods," Cougar told him, blowing a smoke ring at the ceiling. "Besides, it's unreliable. You can beat information out of a feller, but that doesn't mean he'll tell you the truth."

"We've already interrogated Ford and he's been relatively cooperative in the hopes of saving himself from the gallows. That's how we learned what we know about Larson's whereabouts. Perhaps he'll give us the exact location of the Comanchero camp of his own free will."

"And maybe he'll lie through his teeth." Shaddrock snorted. "Besides, that won't help us much. Finding Larson is only part of the problem—and a mighty small part considering we also have to take on fifty men to get those Gatlings."

"I don't see what other use Ford can be." The colonel shrugged.

"How bad is he wounded?" Cougar asked.

"His arm is broken and there's been considerable muscle damage that will probably render the limb useless for the rest of his miserable life."

38

"But he can still walk?" Shaddrock inquired. "Is he fit to travel?"

"What are you thinking of, Mr. Shaddrock?" Sutton demanded.

"Probably the same thing I am." Cougar grinned.

"A stalking horse." The younger bounty hunter supplied.

His partner nodded. "Figured if you rode with me long enough you'd learn *something* eventually."

"You can't seriously be suggesting I release Ford on the chance that you two can follow him to the Comancheros." Sutton shook his head. "Absolutely not!"

"Hell, Colonel." Cougar shrugged. "I thought you wanted Larson and those Gatlings, not some two-bit gun hand with a busted arm."

"But what if he doesn't return to the Comancheros? What if he heads in another direction? Then we'd be no closer to Larson and we might lose the only member of the gang we do have."

"Nobody's saying we should let Ford stroll out of here without an escort," Shaddrock assured him. "We won't lose the bastard and if he doesn't lead us to Larson, we'll bring him back and you'll still have somebody to hang."

"I hope you gentlemen appreciate the position this could put me in if your plan fails."

"It could put us in a pretty serious position too, Colonel," Cougar replied. "Lying face down—dead."

"All right," the officer agreed with a frown. "I'll go along with your plan, providing it isn't too outrageous."

"You haven't given us a chance to explain it yet,"

Shaddrock said.

"First, let me explain something to *you*," Sutton declared as he turned to the map of the Texas-Mexican border. "If Ramon Larson succeeds in selling those guns to his usual customers—bandits, outlaws, hostiles—we'll see a reign of terror throughout the Southwest unlike anything we've ever imagined. The Comancheros could supply small but vicious bands with enough firepower to hold off an entire company of soldiers." He passed a hand over the map. "This area could explode under those conditions. Worse, Larson's success would prompt others to follow his example. Every military train, fortress, and patrol could be under siege. The U.S. Army could be crippled throughout this state."

"We didn't think we were being offered twenty thousand unless the stakes were plenty high," Shaddrock shrugged.

"About the money," the colonel continued. "You'll receive full payment when and *if* you bring in Ramon Larson and the guns."

"Larson may have already sold one or more of the guns," Cougar remarked. "What happens if we can't bring them all back?"

"You'll be paid accordingly. Ten thousand dollars for Larson and roughly fifteen hundred for each of the Gatlings recovered."

"If he's managed to sell enough of those guns, our profit isn't gonna be a helluva lot," Shaddrock complained.

"Those are the conditions," Sutton declared. "Take it or leave it."

Shaddrock turned to his partner. Cougar shrugged. The younger man nodded. "We'll take it."

"One more thing," the colonel warned. "When you go after the Comancheros you're entirely on your own. If you get into trouble in Mexico, don't expect Uncle Sam to bail you out. Officially, there is *no* bounty on Larson or a reward for the guns. We can't allow it to become common knowledge that the United States Army would hire regulators for an illegal mission into a friendly nation, nor can we permit the public to learn that seven Gatlings were stolen from us. Our reputation is at stake."

"So are our lives," Shaddrock muttered sourly.

FOUR

Arlon Ford couldn't sleep. His right arm was still a constant source of discomfort even when he lay on his left side. From time to time he had drifted into slumber and rolled over on the hard bunk. The agony of his damaged limb touching the mattress with his weight on it had forced him awake with a scream on his lips. At times he wished they'd amputated the arm. Perhaps then the pain would go away.

However, the chubby outlaw also suffered from mental torments as well. The Army had charged him with murder, sabotage, stealing government property, and three counts of conspiracy. Ford would sit there in that stinking stockade until the military decided whether to turn him over to a U.S. marshal or execute him themselves. Either way, he was as good as hanged. Sweet Jesus, how did he ever get into such a mess?

The answer came to him as he lay on the cot, with tears of self-pity and pain filling his soft brown eyes. It had all started back in Iowa when he'd fallen in love with Susan Landers. She was the only school teacher in Crawford County, an attractive blonde in her early thirties. Nineteen-year-old Arlon had admired her from afar and longed to be with the schoolmarm.

Then, one day, he gathered up enough courage to ask her to marry him.

A common cowhand for a nearby ranch, Arlon was barely literate and already thirty pounds overweight. Miss Landers rejected his proposal, smiling with amusement at his offer. Something snapped inside the young man's mind. In a maniacal rage of disappointment and anger, he slammed a fist into her pretty face and knocked the teacher down. Then he savagely raped her, biting, punching, and smashing her head into the floorboards until her blond hair was streaked with scarlet. Arlon killed the woman he'd loved—and he'd been stealing, raping, and killing ever since. The incident had created a vicious animal, born of rejection and ridicule.

Now, all the bitterness and anger would end when they slipped a noose around his neck and pulled the lever to the trapdoor of a scaffold. Ford trembled. He didn't want to die, especially that way. Absurdly, he'd felt he was invincible when he rode with the Comancheros. The reality of his own mortality stunned and terrified him as he wept for the wasted life he would soon lose.

"Keep your hands off me, you tin soldier shit!" an angry voice shouted.

"Shut yore mouth, you murderin' bastard!" another snarled while a key turned loudly in a lock.

The door at the end of the corridor opened and two troopers pushed a tall man, dressed in a blue suit and a white Stetson, inside. Alexander Shaddrock pivoted and glared at the soldiers. One of them, a tall, lean sergeant, aimed a Colt .44 at the bounty hunter.

"Try it, dude," he offered. "You killed a friend of mine today. Go ahead and give me a reason to blow yore head off!"

"Your friend called me a card cheat and he went for a gun," Shaddrock replied. "What was I supposed to do? Spill my drink in my lap and ask him to wait until I could change my trousers before he shot me?"

"Joe wasn't armed," the noncom snapped.

"He sure acted like he was carrying a gun." Shaddrock shrugged.

"And you *was* cheatin' at cards too!" the other soldier, a private declared.

"I didn't say the feller was a liar," the regulator commented. "He just wasn't very bright. . ."

The NCO raised his pistol and aimed it at Shaddrock's face. "One more word, sonufabitch! One word!"

"Sergeant Benson," the soldier urged. "Colonel Sutton said you could see to this feller gettin' locked up personal 'cause Corporal Ballanger was a friend o' yore's, but he also said if'n you shot him, you'd better have a mighty good reason."

"I know, Miller," the sergeant hissed. "Unlock Ford's cell. If that Comanchero makes a wrong move, kill him. Even crippled, I don't trust his kind."

"I don't know if we should put them in the same cage . . ."

"You're a private so you don't think period!" Benson snapped. "Maybe these two murderin' scums will kill each other if'n we're lucky. It'd save everybody a heap of trouble."

"Your responsibility, Sergeant," Miller stated as he

44

inserted a key into the cell door.

"Wait a minute," Shaddrock protested. "You aren't throwing me in there with that unwashed lout!"

Miller opened the door and Benson quickly grabbed the lapel of the regulator's jacket and pulled him forward, thrusting the muzzle of his pistol under Shaddrock's chin. Then he shoved the "prisoner," pushing him into the cell. Miller slammed the door and locked it.

"I ain't, huh?" the noncom smiled.

The bounty hunter looked at Ford with distaste and then turned to the soldiers. "There's only one bunk in here. You don't expect me to sleep with this character, do you?"

"Maybe you'll like it." Benson chuckled. "You dress like a sissy anyways."

"Reckon we can go now, Sergeant?" Miller asked hopefully.

"You go ahead," Benson replied, holstering his sidearm. "But give me the keys. I'm stayin' here in case this killer tries anything."

"Colonel Sutton won't like this . . ."

"He told me I don't have to work tomorrow so I'm spendin' the night here to guard this sonufabitch proper!" the NCO growled. "Now git!"

Reluctantly, Private Miller obeyed. The trooper left the stockade. Benson grinned when the door slammed. "You fellers just get comfortable and I'll tell you a nice bedtime story to help you have pleasant dreams."

Ford stared up at the well-dressed stranger, feeling a combination of resentment toward a man who'd obviously lived better than himself and satisfaction that such an individual had been tossed into a cell like a town drunk. He smiled grimly. The fancy dude was going to do a rope dance just like poor white trash Arlon Ford. At least that might be some comfort when they marched him to the gallows.

"Either of you boys ever see a hangin'?" Sergeant Benson began, sitting at an empty apple crate as he removed a tobacco pouch and papers. "I seen about five of 'em. Real interestin'."

"Guess entertainment is difficult to find out here," Shaddrock muttered. He glanced down at Ford as though he didn't even see him and then looked at a small bucket in one corner that served as a latrine.

"They tie yore hands behind yore back before they even let you outta the cell," Benson continued. "Then they escort you down the corridor." He gestured with his freshly rolled cigarette. "Like this one here—and the padre walks along and reads to you outta the Bible. About this time most fellers start to break down. They struggle and fuss, but it don't do no good. You act up too much and you just get the crap beat out of you and they drag you outside anyway."

"I bet you're real popular at parties, fella," the bounty hunter muttered.

"Then they take you up the steps of the gallows. Thirteen of 'em. You might try to brace yore feet against the risers to stop them from takin' you to the top, but it won't help you none. When they gets you to the platform, they bind yore legs together with leather straps so you ain't kickin' all over when they open the trapdoor."

46

"Oh, God!" Ford whined. "Don't say no more!"

"Hell, I ain't told you the good part yet." The sergeant laughed. "They puts the noose over your neck. Sometimes they put a hood on first, but don't count on it. The knot is supposed to be snug against the back o' yore ear so's yore neck'll break when you drop. Don't always work that way. Seen fellers strangle at the end of a rope for more th'n an hour. Tongue sticks out, face turns red, then purple, then black. One time the feller's eyeballs just busted right outta their sockets."

"No!" Ford cried. "No more."

"He hasn't gotten to the punch line yet," the bounty hunter remarked, walking to the bucket in the corner.

"Then, while you're danglin' there a stranglin'," Benson told his literally captive audience, "you lose all control o' yore bodily functions. That means you'll shit yore britches and you'll pee yore pants till it's fillin' up yore boots."

"Speaking of which," Shaddrock interrupted. "This pail is full to the brim with piss and I got some beer still sloshing around in me."

"So let it overflow." Benson chuckled. "I'll let you two clean it up in the morning."

"Generous," the regulator growled as he unbuttoned his fly. "You wouldn't let me out for a while so I could relieve myself without adding to the stink in this place, would you?"

"What do you think, killer?" the sergeant snarled.

"Oh—" Shaddrock sighed, casually strolling back to the barred door— "I think you just might

47

consider it."

Benson's eyes bulged and his mouth fell open when he saw the diminutive .36 caliber single-shot derringer in the bounty hunter's fist.

"What's goin' on?" Ford asked, sliding off the cot.

"I'm getting out of here," Shaddrock snapped. "If you want to go too, you'd better just shut up and do like I tell you."

"You ain't gonna get away with this," Benson said, but his tone lacked any conviction.

"Listen, soldier boy," the bounty hunter sneered. "I managed to slip this little pistol into my pants when you bastards came after me. It's been hurting my crotch for the last half hour and it'll be hurting *yours* if you don't move your butt over here and unlock this cell."

Benson hesitated. Shaddrock cocked the hammer of the derringer. "Castration is just a trigger-pull away, fella," he warned.

"All right," the sergeant declared. "Don't do anything crazy!"

He hurried forward and fumbled with the keys until he inserted the right one and unlocked the cell door. Shaddrock seized the sergeant's tunic front and pulled him into the cell. Taking the Army Colt .44 from Benson's hip holster, Shaddrock gave the derringer to Ford.

"Watch the corridor," the bounty hunter instructed. Then he shoved the muzzle of the revolver into the small of Benson's back. "Over on the bunk, soldier boy."

"What are you going to do?" the sergeant asked

fearfully.

"Take off your cap and jacket," Shaddrock ordered. "Then lie down on your belly. I'm going to tie and gag you."

The NCO obliged. Ford glanced from the corridor to the two men by the cot. He saw Shaddrock raise the Colt overhead and swing it hard. The dull thud of the striking gun butt mingled with Benson's groan. Shaddrock swung the revolver twice more, but the sergeant didn't utter another sound.

"Maybe I'll tell fellas bedtime stories about what it's like to see a man get his head bashed in." The bounty hunter chuckled.

"Hot damn!" Ford smiled. "Is he dead?"

"He might have thought I'd be stupid enough to let him live, but I'm not dumb enough to oblige," Shaddrock replied, tossing his Stetson aside and stripping off his suit coat. He cast a hard glance at Ford. "Keep an eye on that corridor, damn it!"

"What do we do now?" the outlaw inquired.

"We see if we can't just walk out of here together," Shaddrock replied, pulling on Benson's tunic. "Not a bad fit, huh?"

"Them other soldiers will notice you for sure," the Comanchero muttered with a shake of his head.

"Soldiers are a dumb breed . . . what's your name, anyway?"

"Arlon Ford."

"I'm Alexander Shaddrock. Since we're busting out together, it's only right we know who we are. As for my plan, it's the only one we've got—unless you have a better idea, Ford."

49

"I guess we might as well follow yore's, feller." The outlaw sighed. "You done alright so far."

"It'll work," Shaddrock assured him, tugging the brim of the sergeant's cap low over his brow. "I'll play soldier and you just play yourself."

"What if somebody notices you ain't wearin' uniform trousers?"

"Then let's hope we can shoot our way out," the regulator replied flatly.

They emerged from the stockade. Shaddrock hoped Ford wouldn't notice there was no sentry posted outside of the jailhouse. The outlaw didn't seem very bright or observant. He hadn't suspected that the bounty hunter had struck the mattress near Benson's head instead of the sergeant's cranium. So far, so good.

The stars shone coldly in the clear night sky with a bisected moon to cast light upon the fortress below. However, the fugitives could see well enough to discover the parade grounds were deserted. Only the light in a single window suggested anyone was awake except Shaddrock and Ford.

"Sure looks like Lady Luck is with us," Ford whispered.

"Yeah," Shaddrock rasped. "But the cards haven't all been dealt yet."

The pair headed across the grounds, favoring the shadows. Shaddrock didn't fail to notice his companion moved well in the dark, walking with a silent, surreptitious stride unexpected in one of his bulk. The bounty hunter mentally warned himself not to underestimate Ford. He was, after all, a Comanchero and he hadn't been in the stockade for stealing apples from the local parson's tree.

They reached the stables and entered without incident. Shaddrock struck a match and located a kerosene lamp hung on a wall. Ford ground his teeth together and cradled his crippled limb with his good arm, the derringer still in his fist.

"Better not light that thing," the outlaw warned.

"Unless you want to try getting out of here on foot, we're going to have to get a couple of horses," the bounty hunter replied, touching the match to the lamp's wick. "I like to see what I'm stealing and I don't care to ride out of here on some half-dead plow animal or a shavetail mule."

"There's a couple hosses already saddled!" Ford declared with surprise when he saw the two beasts hitched to the rail of a stall.

"No wonder," Shaddrock snorted. "The Morgan is mine. The bastards didn't even bother to take care of him. The piebald must've belonged to the fella I shot. He was a fat slob and that's the biggest pinto I ever saw. Figure he'll do for you?"

"Hell, yes!"

"All right," the regulator nodded. "Let's walk these beasties out of here and hope we can get through the gate without attracting attention."

The pair escorted the horses across the parade field, glancing to and fro for uniformed observers, but the fort remained as silent as a ghost town. At the gate, they stopped to raise the long, heavy bar from the enormous doors. Ford panted heavily from the strain of moving the bolt with only one good arm. Shaddrock pulled one section open as the outlaw led the sturdy Ovaro pinto outside. With some difficulty, Ford managed to haul his obese frame into the saddle. The bounty hunter mounted his horse with almost graceful ease.

"Everything went slicker than owl shit," Ford whispered, a wide grin filling his plump face.

"Halt!" a voice shouted from above. "Who goes there?"

They gazed up at the uniformed sentry who stood on a catwalk on the wall near the gate. He began to raise his Springfield carbine to his shoulder. Shaddrock's arm rose faster. The Army Colt seemed to appear in the bounty hunter's hand as though it sprang from a magician's sleeve. He cocked and fired the pistol. The guard cried out and crumpled from view.

"Jesus!" Ford exclaimed, driving his heels fiercely into the ribs of his mount.

The big Ovaro burst into a gallop. Shaddrock's Morgan followed and soon passed the other horse and rider. The pair rode into the darkness as though the mounted Apocalypse Horsemen were behind them. Colonel Sutton struck a match on one of the erect logs of the open gate and lit a cigar stub while he watched the fugitives depart.

"Sure glad we filled up those prairie dog holes out there," Sergeant Benson remarked as he joined the colonel, his skull intact. "One of those horses might get a busted leg otherwise."

"I just hope those two know what they're doing," Sutton said dryly.

"They probably do, sir," the NCO shrugged. "They just don't know if it'll work or not."

"For crissake!" the guard on the catwalk called down. He rose and placed a hand to the side of his head. "That goddamn regulator's shot came so close the bullet nicked my ear!"

"Don't be upset, soldier," the colonel replied. "I was assured that Shaddrock hits what he aims at—most of the time."

"Reckon he ain't so good at missing," Benson added.

"Mr. Shaddrock had to make his act look real."

"Well, I figure we put on a pretty good show," Sergeant Benson commented. "For a second there, I began to wonder if it wasn't a *real* jail break."

"You did a fine job," Sutton confirmed. "Both of you. It was a convincing performance, but there were a couple of flaws in the script. The bounty hunters said this couldn't be helped. Let's just hope Ford was convinced or Shaddrock and Cougar are getting themselves into a hell of a mess."

Alexander Shaddrock and Arlon Ford rode almost two miles before they slowed their horses to a walk. The bounty hunter sighed with relief. They'd already passed the area he knew to be clear of treacherous rodent burrows and he'd half expected one of their mounts to suffer a crippling fall at any moment.

"Looks like the Army ain't after us yet," Ford remarked.

"They'll probably wait till sunup," Shaddrock said. "Riding is dangerous at night and tracking is damn near impossible."

"Unless they got some Injun scouts. Those red-niggers can sniff out a feller like they was hound dogs. Probably from eatin' so many mutts themselves."

"Biological wonders," the bounty hunter muttered. "There's a forest up ahead. Let's get some rest and move on come dawn."

"You're gonna get all the rest you'll ever need, feller!" Ford declared.

Shaddrock turned to see the muzzle of his own derringer staring back at him. "If you don't want to set up camp here, just say so."

"Plum sorry I have to do this," the outlaw told him, thumbing back the hammer of the tiny pistol. "I'm obliged to you for gettin' me outta that Army fort, but I've got me some plans and I can use every cent I can get. That hoss and saddle of your's will fetch me at least fifty dollars."

"Nothing personal, huh?" Shaddrock glared at him.

"Glad you understand." Ford smiled as he squeezed the trigger.

FIVE

Major Pressman, a small, wiry officer whose uniform was always immaculate with polished brass and shined leather, waited for Colonel Sutton in his office. The major promptly poured some brandy into a balloon glass and placed it on his superior's desk. Sutton wearily nodded his thanks.

"Are they gone, Sir?" Pressman inquired.

"Yes, Major," the colonel sighed. He'd had a long day and Pressman exasperated him at the best of times. The major was a spit-and-polish West Point graduate who'd spent most of his military career behind a desk. He knew paperwork and regulations, but he didn't know men.

"Frankly, sir," the executive officer began, "I think General Andrews made a mistake when he comprised this plan of sending a pair of regulators after those Gatling guns."

"Not *just* a pair of regulators," the colonel corrected. "You've seen the file the general sent us about those two. They're a rather remarkable team if even half of the information is accurate."

"They're unusual to say the least."

"Indeed." Sutton nodded. "Shaddrock comes from one of the best families in Philadelphia. His father is a very successful lawyer. Alexander Shaddrock did well in law school and probably could have followed in the professional footsteps of his father, but he didn't."

"The general believes Shaddrock's family's efforts to select a bride for Alexander prompted him to become something of a black sheep," Major Pressman remarked.

"Whatever the reason," the colonel continued, "Shaddrock joined the Union Army. The war had only recently started and he could have easily acquired a commission with his background and education. He could have spent his time in uniform with a comfortable, safe job as an Army lawyer, handling court martials and never having to worry whether his client won or lost. But he didn't. He enlisted in the infantry as a private."

"Well, he did make a commissioned rank." Pressman shrugged.

"Yes. He *earned* it on the battlefield," Sutton replied. "His commanding officers agree that Lieutenant Shaddrock's courage and daring was exceptional. He received more decorations and honors during his four years of service in the War Between the States than most career men get in a lifetime."

"Not the type you'd expect to find hunting men for bounty rewards," the major admitted. "Cougar seems more the sort for such a sordid profession."

"Thomas Cruthers' background is quite different from Shaddrock's." The colonel nodded. "He's the product of a family of dirt farmers in Arkansas. Apparently he earned his first bounty at the age of seventeen when he shot a chicken thief and later learned

56

the man was a fugitive from a federal prison. As an adult, he didn't do very well at farming and turned professional regulator at the age of twenty. However, when he married, he gave the farm another try, although he continued to hunt men for an additional source of income. Then he captured a killer known as 'the Trumpeter' and held him prisoner at his farmhouse. The captive broke free, shot Cruthers, and murdered his wife, Lydia."

"That's when he turned full-time bounty hunter."

"And he also became more ruthless and cold-blooded," Sutton added. "Since that incident, he hasn't brought in a single wanted man—*alive*. He has yet to kill the wrong man, but he obviously has no qualms about gunning down a guilty one. He generally tries to catch an outlaw in the act of committing a crime to be certain he has the right man . . . or at least a guilty one. In fact, Cruthers has probably killed a great number of human vermin who never had a price on their heads."

"But he was an officer in the Confederate Army."

"That's where he acquired the nickname 'Man Who Hunts Like a Cougar' from the Cherokees in his detachment. Cruthers' experience and cunning earned him promotions rapidly. Don't make the mistake of believing he's an illiterate or ignorant man."

"And his combat record is as impressive as Shaddrock's."

"Yes. If the South had won, Major Cruthers might well have become *General* Cruthers instead of Cougar, the master bounty hunter."

"I wonder how those two ever got together," Pressman mused.

"It happened in the Arizona Territory last year," Sutton explained. "Apparently they both tried to claim the same band of outlaws for a reward at the same time. A partnership developed afterward. Their efficiency as a team was certainly demonstrated in the town of Holden when the pair clashed with that lunatic Colonel Hannibal Brand and his self-styled New Confederacy."

"Judging from the reports, they also crossed swords with a Canadian mercenary and his private trainful of gunmen whom the town had hired for protection from Brand."

"That's beside the point, Major," Sutton replied. "The fact remains that Shaddrock and Cougar singlehandedly took on almost thirty hardened outlaws under that crazy Confederate's command. Do you know of anyone else with such impressive credentials whom we could send after Ramon Larson and his Comancheros?"

"But you *did* send another team of bounty hunters, sir," Pressman reminded the colonel.

"Oh, yes," Sutton nodded. "Schulster, McClean, and Dearn. Those three have something of a reputation in the Southwest—even if they are former outlaws themselves and they're still wanted in Kansas and Missouri for armed robbery and murder. Perhaps they'll succeed if Shaddrock and Cougar fail."

"If they don't *join* the Comancheros instead," Pressman muttered. "Does General Andrews know you called in those three?"

"I didn't see that there was any need to tell him."

Sutton shrugged. "Whichever team of bounty hunters retrieves the Gatlings and brings us Ramon Larson, the Army will still have what it wants. The winner will receive twenty thousand dollars and the loser will get our condolences—that is, if *any* of them come back at all."

"Do Shaddrock and Cougar know about the other three?"

"What would be the point in telling them about their competition?"

"None, I suppose, sir," the major agreed. "Which team do you think will succeed?"

"Probably neither one," Sutton said with a sigh. "If they even find the Comancheros, it's unlikely they'll survive. I've disapproved of this business from the start. Yet, Shaddrock and Cougar do seem far more clever and resourceful than their counterparts. Schulster, McClean, and Dearn have ridden across the border with the intentions of wringing information out of *peones* in the hopes of picking up the Comancheros' trail."

"What do Shaddrock and Cougar plan to do?"

The colonel smiled. "Pour me another brandy and I'll tell you about it, Major."

The derringer clicked harmlessly. Ford's mouth fell open in surprise. Then he realized there was no percussion cap on the nipple at the base of the pistol to ignite powder within the barrel—although he now realized the weapon wasn't loaded either.

"Bang," Shaddrock whispered coldly.

His arm lashed out, swatting the back of his hand

across the outlaw's damaged upper arm hard. Ford cried out and dropped the derringer. He recoiled in the saddle, grasping his pain-racked limb with his hand. A foot slipped from its stirrup and he toppled sideways and fell from the Ovaro to the ground.

"You're a clumsy bastard, Ford," Shaddrock hissed, swinging down from his mount to draw the Army Colt from his belt. "You're also a stupid one. Did you think I'd carry a loaded gun next to my balls?"

"My arm," the outlaw whined.

"That won't be a problem any longer," the bounty hunter assured him, cocking the .44 Colt.

"No!" Ford cried. "Don't . . . please . . ."

"Why not?" Shaddrock demanded. "You were ready to kill me a minute ago, you ungrateful bastard."

"I didn't want to . . ."

"I won't mind killing you at all—*now.*"

"It's just I gotta get back to my gang, that's all," Ford told him.

"Better hope they all go to the sissy section of hell so they can join you, fella."

"Wait!" the outlaw urged. "Maybe we can make a deal."

"What have you got to deal with, fat boy?" Shaddrock sneered.

"I can make you an offer."

"You a pervert as well?"

"Listen, I'm a member of Ramon Larson's gang of Comancheros. Ever hear of them?"

"Sure." Shaddrock nodded. "They're a big outfit

60

that handles some pretty big jobs. What would a little shit like you be doing with them?"

"I'm a Comanchero, damn it!" Ford growled. "If'n you joined up with us, you could be part of the biggest gunrunnin' deal you ever heard of."

"What sort of deal?"

"We stole seven Gatling guns from the Army." The outlaw smiled. "I got caught doin' it, that's how come they had me in that stinkhole jail, but the rest got away. They're down in Mexico and I know where they're holed up."

"Mexico, eh?" Shaddrock mused. "I figure maybe I'd head that way anyhow. After killing two soldiers, I think I'd better avoid showing my face in this country for a while."

"That's right." Ford nodded. "But the cavalry can't do a thing to us if'n we cross the border."

"How do I know old Larson is going to welcome me into the fold? Could be he'll just have my throat slit as soon as we get introduced."

"Larson appreciates a feller with brains. Yore plenty smart, Shaddrock, and you got guts. He'll be glad to have you with us."

"Especially if he has many spineless wonders like you in his gang," Shaddrock declared, easing the hammer of the Colt down. "I'll think about it, but don't try anything again or you're dead. Understand?"

"Sure." Ford bobbed his head woodenly. "We're fellow Comancheros now, so's I figure we . . . ."

"Shut up and lead your horse over to those trees," the bounty hunter told him, stooping to pick up his derringer.

Arlon Ford didn't realize that two guns had been aimed at him that night—Shaddrock's Colt and Cougar's .56 caliber Sharps. Knowing where his partner would take the outlaw, the senior bounty hunter had ridden to the forest and positioned himself among the dense bushes and waited for the pair to arrive.

When he'd seen Ford aim the derringer at Shaddrock's head, Cougar had aimed his buffalo rifle at the Comanchero although he realized the tiny pistol was empty. Cougar felt his stomach muscles knot as he watched the pair from his position among a cluster of bushes a hundred yards away. The regulators hadn't taken the chance of supplying Ford with a loaded weapon, but they hadn't really expected him to try to kill his rescuer.

"Don't make any mistakes tonight, Shaddrock," the bounty hunter whispered. "That son of a bitch is even meaner and more treacherous than we figured."

What disturbed Cougar most was that Arlon Ford was a Sunday School teacher compared to the rest of Ramon Larson's gang—and the bounty hunters would be pitted against fifty Comancheros. If their plan didn't work . . .

Cougar shrugged. *We'll climb into that grave when we get to it.*

SIX

Cougar's concern about his partner proved needless. Shaddrock didn't take any chances with Arlon Ford. He tied the outlaw's hands behind his back and then made a slipknot noose with the rope and dropped it over Ford's head. The Comanchero gasped as Shaddrock slid the knot to the back of his neck.

"I saved you from a hanging," the bounty hunter mused. "Now, if you try to get loose, you'll still wind up dying at the end of a rope. Poetic justice, eh?"

"You've got a sick sense of humor," Ford hissed.

"But the choke will be on you, fella," Shaddrock replied.

"What happens if I move my arms while I'm asleep?" Ford demanded.

"I don't think you'll sleep much," his captor told him, binding the outlaw's ankles together. "That's fair, isn't it? I rescued you and I didn't kill you after you tried to kill me, so you can guard the camp while I rest my brain for a while. No sense in you doing the same since thinking obviously isn't one of your greater accomplishments."

"I hope Larson skins you alive when we get to his headquarters!" Ford snapped.

"Sounds like you're not going to help me join up

63

with the Comancheros," Shaddrock remarked. "I don't really need you then, do I?"

Ford swallowed hard. "I . . . I'm just riled 'cause you hogtied me this way." He smiled nervously.

The bounty hunter glared at him and seriously considered the possibility—even probability—that Arlon Ford would try to encourage Ramon Larson to execute him as soon as they located the Comancheros. Yet Ford remained the only link to the gang and the bounty hunters would have to play the game with the hand they'd dealt themselves. The stakes were twenty thousand dollars and they were gambling with their lives. Hell, that was part of the job, but this time the odds stank.

"Sure hope you calm down by the time we meet up with Larson," Shaddrock declared. "Because if you try to double cross me, you won't live long enough to know if your treachery works."

He walked to the horses and removed the saddles. The regulator poured water from a canteen into the cap he'd taken from Sergeant Benson and allowed the animals to drink from it. "This thing came in useful after all," he commented.

"Lucky them canteens is full," Ford stated. "Looks like you was pretty well supplied."

"I move around a lot," Shaddrock replied.

He draped a blanket over Ford and hauled out his saddle bags. He removed a sheepskin coat and discarded the Army tunic. Nights could be surprisingly cold in Texas. He pulled on the jacket and carried his bags to the small campfire in the center of a clearing.

"How long have you been with the Comancheros,

Ford?" he inquired, untying his bedroll.

"About six months," the outlaw replied. "They're some outfit, I can tell you."

"I'm letting you," Shaddrock assured him. "How many are in the gang?"

"That sort'a varies dependin' on how many fellers gets killed or captured," Ford told him. "But there's always more *bandidos* or hootowls ready to take their places. Sometimes there's about forty men, sometimes sixty or more."

The bounty hunter managed to keep his features from betraying his consternation. *Sixty or more!* "I always figured the Comancheros were mostly Mexicans and such. How'd you manage to get in with them?"

"Hell, Larson is half *gringo* himself, although he don't care much for 'em. He still hires on any *Americano* he figures has all the necessary talents."

"Like you?" Shaddrock snorted. "Some outfit!"

Ford's eyes narrowed. "How about Wesley Quint?"

The regulator looked at him with surprise. "Quint? The pistolman?"

"That's right," the outlaw grinned. "Seems a while back he caught a bullet from somebody nearly as fast as him—and there ain't *nobody* faster. Believe me. I've seen him gun down five men quicker than you can cock the hammer o' yore gun. Ain't natural. Still, I reckon he figured gunfightin' was too risky a business. Even when you kill the other feller he might manage to put a couple in you a'fore he knows he's dead."

"So he turned Comanchero?"

Ford nodded. "He's Ramon's right hand man now.

Got a couple other *Anglos* too, but most of the gang is greaser bandits and half-breeds. Anything with mixed blood ain't welcome nowheres, north or south of the border by white man or red—except among the Comancheros."

"Old Larson's got himself a regular sanctuary for the downtrodden," the bounty hunter scoffed. "Well, right now, I guess that category fits us too."

He lay on his bedroll and pulled a blanket to his chin. The saddle bags he used for a pillow were far from comfortable because they contained his twin Police Colts, loaded with caps, balls, and powder. The bounty hunter wanted his untrustworthy companion to believe the only weapons he had were the .44 Army revolver and the empty derringer. There is never any advantage in allowing an enemy to know one's full strength. The less Ford suspected, the better. With the comforting knowledge that he had a hidden arsenal and that his partner watched over him, Shaddrock drifted into a sound sleep of one accustomed to danger.

Cougar, also clad in a sheepskin coat but without the benefit of a blanket and fire, watched the camp most of the night. He had slept for a couple of hours before assuming his vigil. The senior bounty hunter had learned that patience was as much a tool of his profession as a man stalker as a reliable firearm and good reflexes. He smiled, thinking of the Alexander Shaddrock he'd known a year before. Reckless, bold, and foolhardy, the young Easterner had learned a lot about his chosen trade. He was more cautious now and less apt to take unnecessary chances—at least most of the time.

Yet, Shaddrock would always be the more impetuous of the pair. He had volunteered to take the lion's share of the risk by playing the role of fellow fugitive to lead them to the Comancheros. Fine. Cougar was better suited as the "outside man." He knew how to track and he had the patience and experience to handle the long hours, days—possibly weeks—of surveillance without exposing himself to the enemy. To Cougar, war had been bounty hunting and bounty hunting was war. The men he stalked were foes, vicious human varmints like the murderous animal who'd killed his Lydia. They were a threat to everything decent and gentle, kind and good—all the things Lydia had been.

He felt moisture accumulate in his dark eyes as he recalled her. The only woman he'd ever loved. Long years had passed, yet his memories of her were as vivid and dazzling as the noon sun. She had been beautiful, bright, and full of life. The only true happiness he'd ever known had been with her. They'd had so little time together, yet they'd shared so much. Now she was gone.

In a sense, Thomas Cruthers had also died that night when the Trumpeter pumped two .31 caliber bullets into his wife's brain. Cougar had taken his place. The man who hunted like his namesake, the big cat—cunning, merciless, and alone.

Until he'd met Shaddrock.

How the hell had they become partners? The senior bounty hunter couldn't rightly recall when they'd turned from a pair of quarreling competitors to a functional team. The young Yankee romantic and the battlescarred Reb cynic had somehow become partners and friends.

Cougar roughly brushed a tear from his cheek with a knuckle. He had a job to do and sentimental bullshit wasn't part of it. They were pursuing a terrific bounty, and Shaddrock—that magnificent jackass—was taking an enormous chance so they could acquire it. Once before, Cougar had failed in his vigilance and Lydia had died because of it. That wouldn't happen again—*ever.*

Arlon Ford hadn't tried to escape. He hadn't managed to get any sleep either due to the threat of strangulation and the constant ache of his maimed arm. Once, he'd shouted curses at his companion and captor, determined to rob the bounty hunter of the rest he was unable to enjoy. Shaddrock simply told the outlaw if he disturbed him again there'd better be a good reason or he'd find out how well Ford's teeth could endure a couple swats of a gun barrel. Ford had remained silent until the other man awoke at daybreak.

"All right, partner," Cougar whispered wearily. "You're on your own for a while. Don't get yourself killed."

With that, he stretched out under the shade of a tree, pulled the wide brim of his Montana peak hat over his eyes, and slept. The sawed-off Greener lay by his right side and the Sharps by his left, a hand resting on each weapon. It was how he always slept on the trail—and he couldn't rest easily any other way.

"Can I talk now?" Ford growled, watching Shaddrock stretch the slumber from his body.

"Sure," the bounty hunter assured him. "A little conversation before breakfast is always a nice way to begin the day."

"You're a fuckin' son of a bitch!" the outlaw snarled.

"I can see you're out of sorts until you've had your first cup of coffee," Shaddrock replied mildly. "Don't get up. I'll see to it," he told the still bound Ford.

The bounty hunter carried his saddle bags to the horses and removed his jacket. Standing beyond his prisoner's view, Shaddrock took his shoulder holsters from the bags and slipped into them. Filling the leather with his Police Colts, he pulled on the sheepskin coat and rummaged through his gear for coffee, pot, and canteen.

"Will sour dough biscuits and sardines be all right with you?" he called. "The chicken didn't lay any eggs this morning."

"Just untie me, you bastard!" Ford demanded.

"I'll get around to it," the regulator assured him. "How long do you think it'll take to get to Larson's camp?"

"If we spend all morning talkin', the goddamn soldiers will find us first!" the Comanchero snapped.

"I don't think so," Shaddrock replied, well aware the Army didn't want any contact with them now. Besides, Cougar would be sleeping for two-hour intervals while he followed them and the more time they spent at the camp, the easier for him to pick up their trail later.

"We should be there this afternoon," Ford muttered sourly. "Four or five o'clock maybe."

"Fine," the bounty hunter replied. "You say Larson stole some Gatling guns. What's he plan to do with them?"

"Sell 'em, of course." Ford shrugged.

"Who to?"

"Larson has connections." The outlaw smiled. "He knows where to get top dollar for them guns. He's already settin' up the deals by now. Pretty soon those Gatlings will be scattered among outlaw gangs, *bandidos,* and Injuns all over this state and Mexico and maybe the Arizona Territory as well."

And there goes half our bounty, Shaddrock thought sourly.

The pair crossed the border early that afternoon. Despite the heat, Shaddrock still wore his sheepskin coat, unbuttoned with the walnut grips of the Army .44 visible in his belt, although the Police Colts in shoulder leather remained out of sight. The bounty hunter and Arlon Ford traveled into the arid plains of Mexico, surrounded by miles of mesquite, cactus, and sand. The scenery didn't change until they approached a great cluster of boulders.

The rock formations had been there for millions of years. Originally formed beneath the sea, the stone monuments had remained when the waters drew back and the continents appeared. Unknown thousands of years passed. The elements had altered the shapes of the rocks, yet they had withstood the ravages of time, silent gray guardians of a changing planet.

However, Ramon Larson and the Comancheros were a relatively recent addition. A sombrero clad sentry among the boulders announced the approaching riders. Fifteen armed men emerged from their positions among the rocks to receive the unexpected visitors.

"Don't act rashly, fellers," Ford urged, first in English and then very crude Spanish. "You don't want to shoot an *amigo*, eh?"

"Ford?" questioned Juan Alverez, a tall former *bandido*, who favored flashy red clothing with silver trimmings. "We thought you were dead or a prisoner of the anglo Army."

"I *was* their prisoner," the outlaw replied. "With the help of this man, I managed to escape to return here."

"Really?" Alverez smiled, revealing a gold tooth among the tobacco-stained real ones. "Such loyalty is commendable, no?" He aimed a Colt revolver at the pair.

Shaddrock watched the Comancheros with apprehension. He had never encountered a group of men as savage or wicked in appearance as the collection before him. They wore an assortment of clothing, mostly dirty and patched. All were heavily armed with one or more pistols and knives. Most carried a rifle or carbine.

"Hell, Juan." Ford smiled nervously. "Ain't no need to point that gun at us."

"No?" Alverez replied. "Your friend carries a *pistola*. I think he should take it out very slowly and drop it to the ground as a gesture of friendship."

71

The bounty hunter sighed and drew the Army Colt from his belt. "There's a round under the hammer. Suppose I hand it to one of you fellas to avoid any accidents?"

"That is a careless way to carry a gun, *señor,*" Alverez commented. "Didn't anyone ever tell you the firing pin should be resting on an empty chamber?"

"Sure did," Shaddrock replied. "But I didn't get around to adjusting the cylinder of this revolver since I shot one of the soldiers when we made our break last night."

"We shall see what Ramon thinks about this miracle escape, *gringo,*" the ex-bandit snorted. He turned to the others. *"Vamanos!"*

The Comancheros "welcome wagon" escorted the newcomers through a division in the rock formations. The stone walls formed a natural circle of boulders around a large clearing. A number of canvas tents had been erected and campfires heated pots of coffee and chili. Other Comancheros, as dirty and menacing as the first group, watched the procession with expressions of interest, suspicion, or amusement. Their verbal remarks were equally varied, consisting of snickers, shouts, and muttered comments.

The flap of the largest tent, near the center of the bivouac area, parted and a slender figure dressed in a white shirt, *vaquero* trousers, and boots emerged. Shaddrock noticed the cutlass sword thrust through the man's red sash and realized he was looking at Ramon Larson himself. The man with a ten thousand dollar price on his head.

"You're all making enough noise to disturb my sex

72

with Marie," the Comanchero leader complained. "She is most upset to have her pleasures interrupted. The reason for this had better be good."

"Arlon Ford has returned," Alverez explained.

"That is hardly worth all this." Larson frowned.

"But he was captured by the soldiers, Ramon," the ex-*bandido* replied. "And he has come back with a stranger who helped him escape."

"Si." Larson nodded, glancing up at Shaddrock. "Another *gringo,* of course."

"If you hate us *gringos* you'll have to hate half of yourself too," Wesley Quint remarked with a wry grin. The hatchet-faced killer strolled casually to his boss, a hand draped over the butt of his Smith & Wesson in its low hung holster.

"I *do* hate the anglo blood in my veins," the Comanchero hissed. "The *bastardo* left my mother as one would a common *puta.* So do not expect me to be proud of his name."

"I ain't your daddy," Quint said sharply. "Neither is this feller."

"Si," Larson admitted. "If he *was* here I would have the pleasure of putting a bullet in his head." The Comanchero chief watched Shaddrock dismount. "Ford is not smart enough to pick his nose without instructions, so *if* the two of you escaped from a *gringo* jail, you must have done most of the mental work, *señor...?"*

"Shaddrock," the bounty hunter answered as he stepped closer. "And you might say I led your boy here by the hand when we left Fort McCullen. Then the son of a bitch tried to kill me so I had to tie him up

73

last night. He might still be upset about that."

"Why did you spare his life, Shaddrock?" Larson asked.

"So I could see about a job with you fellas." The regulator shrugged. "Until now, I figured he was probably telling me a pack of lies, but . . ."

"Ford!" Larson snapped suddenly.

Shaddrock whirled to see the fat outlaw had snatched a carbine from the grasp of an unsuspecting Comanchero. Ford aimed the gun at the bounty hunter, a fierce expression etched on his round face.

"This is for treatin' me like a fuckin' animal, you bastard!" he snarled, cocking the lever action of the weapon.

A dozen guns swung toward Arlon Ford, but the Comancheros hesitated, uncertain if their leader would approve of shooting Ford to save the life of an anglo stranger. However, one hand did not consider Larson's wishes and reacted instantly, drawing a revolver, aiming, cocking, and firing in a fast smooth continuous motion.

The .36 caliber lead ball struck the brass frame of the Henry carbine in Ford's fists, ricocheting upward to smash into the outlaw's jaw. Bone and teeth shattered. The impact of the slug knocked the dazed Comanchero backward. A Police Colt in Shaddrock's right hand roared again as he drew the other pistol with his left. The second round struck Ford in the center of the chest and the third bullet, fired from the other Colt, drilled a hole an inch below the latter.

Arlon Ford released the carbine and staggered three steps before he fell. An expression of total astonishment was frozen on his lifeless features as his face stared up at the sun without comprehension.

The Comancheros abruptly trained their weapons on Shaddrock. The bounty hunter lowered his pistols and turned to Ramon Larson.

"That Ford always was a back shooter," the Comanchero leader remarked with a shrug.

"He used to brag that one of his cousins is associated with the James Boys," Quint mused. "Wonder if it runs in the family." He looked at Shaddrock. "Pretty fair shootin', feller."

"Ford was a big target," the regulator replied simply.

"Since our fat friend can no longer tell us what happened at the Army fort," Larson remarked. "You'll have to tell us, Shaddrock. If you can convince me I shouldn't have you shot, perhaps I'll let you live awhile."

"I killed a soldier who accused me of cheating at cards," the bounty hunter answered. "The Army locked me up, but they didn't know I had a derringer tucked away. That's how I convinced the jailer to let us go."

"Mighty good at hidin' guns, ain't you?" Quint smiled.

"It comes in handy," Shaddrock replied. "Anyway, I bashed in the fella's head, then Ford and I helped ourselves to a couple horses. The Morgan belonged to me before the Army took it and it still had my Colts and shoulder holsters in the saddle bags."

"Sounds too easy," Alverez muttered with suspicion.

"It wasn't," Shaddrock told him. "But it wasn't complicated either. The more complex a plan is, the more likely something will go wrong. Besides, I hadn't expected to get thrown in jail. It was the best I could do on short notice."

"Well, Ford didn't have any close friends, so no one is going to want to avenge him and we recently lost a couple men," Larson declared. He turned to his followers. "Do we let this *Anglo* stay with us for a while and decide if he deserves to join us—or should he join *señor* Ford?"

Voices replied eagerly in Spanish, English, and Yaqui. Several expressed an unwillingness to accept the newcomer, but the majority approved of his temporary enlistment.

"Congratulations, *gringo*," the Comanchero leader remarked. "You get to live—at least for a little while."

"That's very generous of you," the bounty hunter replied dryly.

"Reckon nobody'll mind if'n I keep Ford's pinto," Jethro Mackall remarked, fondling the handle of the bullwhip draped around his neck like a pet serpent. "Do we let this feller have his hoss?"

"*Seguro*," Larson confirmed. "But I think it would be a good idea for *señor* Shaddrock to surrender his firearms for the time being."

"That *isn't* so generous," the regulator muttered.

Twilight claimed the sky and the Comancheros relaxed in a manner suited to their kind. They opened bottles of tequila and whiskey as they sat around campfires and exchanged tales of bold deeds and sex-

76

ually adept women. Several Mexicans sang ballads, most flavored with Spanish profanity. An argument between a Yaqui half-breed and an ex-*bandido* grew heated until both men pulled knives.

The other Comancheros laughed at the combatants' awkward drunken slashes and stabs, cheering their favored man in the contest and booing when his blade failed to connect with the opponent. When the Yaqui's knife ripped open the Mexican's shirt and drew first blood, Larson's amusement ceased. He ordered Luis to end the fight before a serious injury occurred. The towering Mexican hulk grinned, happy to oblige. Luis moved behind the half-breed and slammed a big fist into the back of his head. The Yaqui fell unconscious and his adversary soon joined him when Luis punched him on the chin.

Other Comancheros chose different diversions. One tent housed five prostitutes. Although fat and aged by their profession, the women serviced any lustful outlaw who decided to indulge in sexual intercourse. They fornicated like field animals, all joining inside the tent, grunting, groping, and sweating in the confined area. Occasionally two or more men would have the same woman simultaneously, but none fought over the haggard, hardened whores. They weren't worth the effort.

A few gang members elected to quietly drink themselves into a stupor and sleep. The men on sentry duty, however, didn't touch anything stronger than coffee. Larson posted six men to guard the bivouac area and they all took the task seriously, well aware that their leader would deal harshly with anyone who failed to remain alert.

Cougar took note of all these activities as he watched the camp from his position on a rocky hill a quarter of a mile away. Shielding his field glasses with his hat to avoid reflecting moonlight on the lenses, he scanned the area until he located Shaddrock seated on a small keg. His partner grimaced at the taste of raw tequila as he lowered a bottle. Cougar shifted the glasses and found two large wagons near the edge of the camp. Likely transportation for the Gatlings, but where did Larson have the guns now?

The bounty hunter put down the fieldglasses and reached for some beef jerky in his pocket. Suddenly, he realized a large shape had blotted out the sky beside him. Mentally cursing himself for failing to pay attention to his immediate surroundings, Cougar tried to roll away from the intruder and clawed at the Bowie knife in his belt. Even before he saw the gleam of gun metal flash, he knew he'd reacted too late. The barrel of the revolver crashed into his skull and the world exploded into a blinding snowstorm of white agony—followed by the blackness of oblivion.

SEVEN

"How do you like my little family, *gringo?*" Ramon Larson inquired as he sat down on a crate beside Alexander Shaddrock.

"I'd like it better if papa quit calling me *gringo,*" the bounty hunter replied flatly, his cool blue eyes gazing steadily into the Comanchero's dark orbs.

"Bueno!" Larson declared with a smile. "You speak your mind, *señor.* Most of these *estupidos* have too little mind or too little guts to do so."

"Maybe they're just inarticulate." Shaddrock shrugged.

"Si." Larson nodded. "Most of them cannot read."

The regulator pointed at the sentries among the rocks. "Do you always post so many guards?"

"Not always," the Comanchero answered. "But tonight there is a chance we might get a visit from the Army, no?"

"I doubt that the U.S. cavalry would cross the border just to catch two fugitives," the bounty hunter commented. "Ford and I would hardly be worth the risk of violating another country's boundaries."

"Perhaps," Larson allowed. "And perhaps the *gringos* and the *Federales*—or more likely, the *rurales*—have made a deal. They have no love for

Comancheros either, Shaddrock."

"And you think I helped Ford escape so he could lead them here?"

"It is possible."

"It's also unnecessary," Shaddrock snorted, "I heard a couple soldiers talking about the Comancheros back at Fort McCullen. It seems your boy Ford told them everything he knew, including the location of this camp, to try to save his neck. The boys in blue were pretty pissed off because the gang was on the other side of the border. What the hell would they need me for if they planned to team up with the Mexican authorities?"

"That's what you say, Shaddrock." Larson shrugged. "But do not be concerned. If I really felt the Army had sent you, you would already be dead. Still, do not expect too much trust too soon."

"Trust takes a while to earn," the bounty hunter agreed. "Just don't kill me until I get a chance to do so."

"That will be up to you, Shaddrock," the Comanchero replied with a grin.

The flap of Larson's tent opened as the bounty hunter's gaze wandered in that direction. His eyes widened with appreciation when he saw the shapely figure at the threshold. She was tall and gracefully lean, yet her breasts and hips were voluptuously full. The woman's alabaster complexion and delicate features seemed out of place in the arid Mexican plains. Although her long hair was blood-red, the girl's high cheekbones suggested a trace of Cherokee in her ancestry. A silk nightgown with a plunging neckline offered a generous view of cleavage, and the outline beneath the thin cloth hinted of the contours of her body.

"Ramon," she said in a sensuously husky voice. "How much longer will it be before you return to my bed?"

"When I have seen to my men, *novia*," Larson replied gruffly.

"But I yearn for your manhood within me." She pouted. "No woman should have to suffer the torment of waiting for one as *macho* as you—if another man remotely close to you exists."

"There isn't, Marie." Larson chuckled. "Be patient. I will make it worth waiting for."

"You always do." The woman smiled.

With a sigh, the Comanchero leader rose and walked to another tent. Marie's jade green eyes met Shaddrock's. He treated her to a boyish grin and she responded with a wide smile.

"The night chill cuts to the bone," the woman said, hugging herself, her arms pushing under her breasts, increasing the swell of her bosom.

"Don't you have something to wrap around yourself, ma'am?" the bounty hunter inquired.

"What would you suggest?" she replied coyly.

"I could fetch you a horse blanket."

Her smile faded. "Some of that tequila might be better."

"Of course," he agreed, carrying the bottle as he walked closer. "Sorry I can't offer you a glass."

"A man of breeding and manners," she said scornfully. "You are the new man, right? Shamrock?"

"*Shaddr*ock," he corrected, offering the tequila to

her. "Why don't you call me Alex?"

"Very well," Marie agreed. She raised the tequila bottle to her lips and gulped down the fiery liquid as though it were well water. "How did you come to join *this* bunch?" She gestured with a hand to indicate the entire camp.

"What's a nice boy like me doing in a place like this, eh?" Shaddrock grinned. "Well, I killed three soldiers and broke out of an Army stockade up north, so I guess I qualify."

"I saw you shoot Fatty Ford too," she remarked. "That's a sure sign of a Comanchero—when you don't mind killing your friends."

"My friends don't try to put a bullet in my back."

"Well, you may make some friends here—if you live long enough."

"I'm sort of particular about who I get close to," Shaddrock told her.

"Is that why you aren't at the *puta* palace over there?" She pointed at the tent containing the prostitutes.

"I like a little privacy," the bounty hunter replied. "And I'm fastidious about my women."

"Have you had many women?" She raised an eyebrow.

"I can always use one more," he assured her. "If she's the right woman."

"Perhaps we should talk about this later, Alex," Marie said, holding out the almost empty bottle.

"You keep it," he urged. "A gift."

"How chivalrous."

"That's me. Sir Alexander of King Ramon's court."

82

She laughed. "Have a good night, good knight."

With that, Marie returned to the tent. Shaddrock hummed softly with expectation of future meetings as he turned. A long steel blade rose suddenly to his chin. The bounty hunter inhaled sharply and shifted his eyes to the face behind the sword.

"There are three things a wise man does not do, Shaddrock," Ramon Larson warned. "He does not steal anything that isn't worth taking, he doesn't shoot a man unless he intends to kill him and he doesn't go near my *mujer.*"

"She said she was cold, so I gave her that bottle to warm her insides with tequila," Shaddrock told him, glaring back at the Comanchero's angry features. "After she drinks that shitty stuff she'll probably want to kill me herself. Save your threats for someone who deserves them, Ramon—and get that fucking thing away from me."

"Ah, you do have *huevos*—balls." Larson grinned as he slid the cutlass into his sash. "But don't exercise them too much or I may have to cut them off, no?"

"You don't need any extras, do you, Ramon?" Shaddrock replied dryly, walking past the Comanchero leader.

Cougar's eyelids parted slowly, painfully, as consciousness returned. His head throbbed dully and his mouth felt as though a cowpie had been stuffed into it, but his mind still recalled all vital information—such as who he was and what he had been doing before the blow to the skull occurred. Gradually, his body sent messages to his brain. The constriction and numbness at his wrists and ankles told him he'd been bound. His vision cleared, but the sour taste remained. A dirty rag had been tied around his mouth as a gag.

Oh, shit, he thought, scanning his surroundings. The bounty hunter was lying on a dirt floor within a small adobe structure. Flimsy furniture of wired wood had been pushed to one side and bloodstained blankets lay on a pile of straw. Two men stood in the center of the room, their height and size exaggerated by Cougar's prone point of view. One seemed to be nine feet tall, his lean build obvious despite a bulky, soiled cattleman's frock that hung on him like a canvas tarp. His battered ten-gallon hat contributed to the illusion of height. The other man was a mere eight feet and a half, his paunchy belly hanging over a gunbelt and his round face covered by dense brown whiskers.

"Looks like ye didn't hit 'im too hard after all, Mac," Jake Schulster, the fat regulator commented.

Townsend "Mac" McClean grinned, revealing large yellow teeth. "Hit 'im pretty hard though. Feller sure moved quick once he knew I was thare. Almost missed his noggin entirely."

"Seein' as how he was usin' them fieldglasses to watch Larson's camp, I don't reckon he's no Comanchero," Schulster mused.

The tacked-on door of the adobe hut opened, and a broadshouldered figure with a small oval head entered. "I dumped them dead greasers far enough from here so's we don't have t' smell their stink," Fred Dearn announced, cradling a Spencer carbine under his arm.

"That's good work, Fred," Schulster assured him, speaking to his partner as one might a slow-witted child. "Now, you jus' stay outside and watch in case any of 'em badmen comes 'round."

"Out by the rocks?" Dearn inquired.

"That's right." Schulster nodded.

The feeble-minded regulator grinned. "We gonna kill that feller, Jake?"

"We're gonna have a talk with 'im first," the leader of the trio replied. "You go watch for them bad fellers and keep alert. We'll let you know when we're ready to kill 'im."

Dearn giggled as he left the hut. McClean held Cougar's gunbelt and examined it with interest. "Whoever we got here, he sure ain't no saddle bum out for a stroll," the bounty hunter remarked. "This rig is a professional's. Holster set low, leather waxed on the inside, and a slit along the top so's the gun'll come out quick as a rattler."

"Yeah," Schulster agreed. "And the sights o' his Dragoon pistol is special' made 'n adjusted. Hammer's been widened by a gunsmith so's it can be cocked easier and I figure that Colt's got a hair trigger as well."

"That Sharps is a damn good gun too," McClean added. He drew Cougar's Bowie knife. "And ye notice how this toad sticker is in the sheath so's it can be pulled out fast. Got ourselves a mean feler here."

"And I think I know who it is." Schulster smiled. "Only one feller I heard o' who's an expert pistolman, knife fighter, rifle marksman, and uses a sawed-off Greener as well . . . Thomas Cruthers."

85

"Cougar?" McClean's mouth fell open. "Jesus, he's supposed to be the best bounty hunter in the whole goddamn West!"

"That must be bullshit." Schulster chuckled. " 'Cause we got 'im, didn't we? Reckon that means we're number one now!"

Cougar sat up slowly. Although his head had cleared and his senses now functioned at their peak level, he squinted his eyes and groaned through the gag. He didn't waste time chiding himself for getting captured by the trio of regulators. What had happened couldn't be erased, so he'd simply have to deal with the reality of the present situation the best he could.

Fortunately, his captors had made two mistakes. First, they'd tied his hands in front of him instead of behind his back and second, they'd failed to notice the bulge at the inside of the deerskin boot on his left foot. Dearn had probably bound his ankles. However, if Cougar was going to survive, he couldn't afford to make *any* mistakes.

"Well, he's comin' to," McClean declared. "How 'bout it, mister? You that big, bad Cougar feller we done heard is supposed to be so unbeatable? You shore don't look so big now!"

"He's Cougar alright," Schulster declared. "That explains why he was here. The gawddamn Army done hired him as well as us and didn't bother to mention it. Fuckers must be plannin' to pay whoever brings in them Gatlin's first."

"Well, I ain't gonna share no twenty thousand dollar reward with this sonufabitch," McClean growled.

"Course not," Schulster agreed. "And I don't want to take no chances with him. Cougar didn't get his reputation by being sissy."

"Figure there's anything to gain by questionin' 'im?"

"Hell, he don't know anymore 'bout them Comancheros than we do. He's nothin' but competition."

"So we get rid of 'im." McClean tested the edge of Cougar's Bowie with his thumb.

"Right," Schulster confirmed, drawing a double-edged Arkansas Toothpick from a sheath on his hip. "We'll do it quiet like—same way we kilt that Mex family that was in this hut a'fore we moved in."

"Fred's gonna be disappointed that he missed seein' this," McClean mused as they approached their bound prisoner.

"He'll get to kill a lot of fellers soon enough," Schulster replied. "But since we're so close to Larson's campsite, I want one o' us standin' guard at all times."

"Makes sense," the other regulator agreed. "Besides, why should a peabrain like Fred get any credit for killin' the famous Mr. Cougar?"

With another groan, their prisoner rolled to one side, turning his back to them and curling his body into a ball. The pair snickered, unaware that Cougar's bound hands reached to the weapon hidden in his boot. He pulled the compact, slender Hopkins and Allen pistol from the deerskin and cocked the unusual hammer, located behind the trigger guard. Rolling to face them, Cougar raised the boot gun and fired into the astonished features of Jake Schulster. The man's

87

face disappeared into scarlet pulp, the back of his skull erupting like a tiny volcano, spitting blood, brains, and shattered bone.

Before Townsend McClean could recover from the shock of the unexpected gunshot and the sight of his partner's exploding head, Cougar hurled himself into the tall bounty hunter's legs. McClean cried out as his feet were bowled out from under him. He fell to all fours, but swiftly slashed the Bowie at his still-bound opponent. Cougar sat up and swung the now-empty Hopkins & Allen. The iron barrel smashed into the other bounty hunter's wrist, knocking the knife from numbed fingers.

McClean grunted, glared at his adversary, and then launched himself at Cougar. The senior bounty hunter rolled onto his back and drew his knees to his chest, allowing his opponent to close in. Then he launched both feet upward, driving the heels of his boots into McClean's face. The regulator's head snapped back, blood issuing from his smashed mouth. He slumped to the floor unconscious.

"Right now, *you* don't look so big, Mac," Cougar muttered as the gag worked loose. He quickly crawled to the discarded Bowie.

Grabbing the familiar staghorn handle of his knife, Cougar inserted the blade into the ropes at his wrists and sawed through them. The door burst open a second later. Fred Dearn appeared at the threshold, his Spencer carbine held ready.

"Jake? Mac?" the dull-witted bounty hunter asked before he saw his partners sprawled on the floor.

Cougar held the Bowie by the tip of its blade and

raised it to his ear as Dearn swung the Spencer toward him.

"You killed them, you bastard!" he bellowed, putting the butt stock to his shoulder.

The senior bounty hunter threw the knife before Dearn could pull the trigger. The Bowie spun one and a half times, then slammed point-first into the big man's chest. Dearn screamed and fired the Spencer. A big .52 caliber slug crashed into the dirt floor near Cougar. But Fred Dearn didn't live long enough to try again.

The simple-minded regulator dropped the carbine and clawed at the handle of the Bowie that jutted from his blood-splashed shirt. His stupid face seemed to acquire sudden intelligence as his brow wrinkled in concentration. Perhaps he learned something profound about death a moment before it claimed him. Dearn stumbled through the doorway and fell to the ground outside.

Cougar sighed with relief. "That takes care of those three," he rasped. "Now all I have to worry about are the fifty Comancheros who sure as hell heard those shots."

EIGHT

The celebration within the Comanchero camp ended abruptly. Several members had passed out and others responded drunkenly, clumsy hands groping for holstered sidearms they no longer wore. Most, however, were sober enough to react like trained soldiers. They quickly seized their weapons and moved into prearranged positions throughout the camp. Ramon Larson, silverplated pistol in hand, ran to the tent nearest the gap in the rock formations that led into the bivouac area.

"Move your *nalgas!*" he shouted at the men within.

The large multibarreled muzzles of a Gatling gun poked through the canvas flap. Shaddrock watched as three Comancheros set up the rapid fire weapon by the camp's threshold. Another Gatling was hauled out and placed at a different angle to guard the gap. Wesley Quint supervised other teams of Comancheros who carried Gatlings up to the rocks and put the guns in position for a vicious cross fire in case invaders managed to penetrate the area.

The bounty hunter noted the smooth efficiency of the gang. They responded well, instantly assuming their roles in the preparations—obviously they were well-trained and well-drilled. He warned himself not to underestimate these men. Their appearance, uncouth manners, and brutish behavior didn't prevent them from operating like a top-notch military unit under stress. He recalled his own poor joke about "extraordinary-cheros." Whatever term one gave Larson's men, they were far more than an "average" gang of outlaws.

At least now he knew the Comancheros still had the Gatling guns. He counted five of the stolen weapons, which left two unaccounted for. Larson either had them in another tent for a last-ditch defense or he'd already sold the guns. How the hell were they going to get seven or even five Gatlings away from the Comancheros and across the border?

Worst of all, Shaddrock knew Cougar was out there—somewhere beyond the campsite and it seemed probable he'd been involved in the shooting. Roughly half the gang were already saddling horses to investigate the shots. Could the senior bounty hunter successfully hide from that many men—assuming he was still alive?

"Shaddrock!" Wesley Quint snapped gruffly, leading a black mare and the regulator's Morgan by their reins. Both animals were saddled. "Get on your horse. You're coming with us!"

"Sure," the bounty hunter agreed. "Do I get my guns too?"

"Hell, no," the gunfighter growled. "I supported you joinin' our little group 'cause you're a fellow American and there ain't many here, but if'n we find an Army patrol out there, I'm gonna kill you myself for leadin' them here!"

"If there's one out there," Shaddrock replied, climbing into the saddle. "It's none of my doing—unless they tracked Ford and me this far."

"You'd better hope we don't find no uniformed bastards then, feller," Quint warned.

Ramon Larson stayed behind at the campsite while his second in command led eighteen men from the rock walls to investigate the sounds. Quint had obviously acquired a great deal of respect among the Comancheros. There was no grumbling or complaints among the Mexican and half-breed members when they had to take orders from the *gringo*. No one hesitated when he told them to fan out in a horseshoe formation and ride to the northwest—the direction the shots had come from.

Weapons ready, they soon located a small adobe hut less than a quarter mile from the Comanchero headquarters. The gang surrounded the tiny structure, closing their semicircle like the jaws of a great beast. Quint rode beside Shaddrock, watching the bounty hunter via the corner of his eye. Shaddrock was one of half a dozen riders who'd been ordered to carry a lantern to illuminate the path for the others. He wondered if his fellow lamp-bearers felt as uneasy as he did at being a prime target for any hidden sharpshooters in or around the hut.

"Jethro, Gomez, Miguel, Shaddrock," Quint called out. "Come with me. The rest of you keep us covered."

The gunfighter and his chosen men eased their horses forward and gradually approached the structure. From its crumbling adobe and reed-covered roof, they realized it was the home of a peasant family. Goats and sheep bleated nervously within a poorly built corral as the riders drew closer. Four horses were hitched to the fence, including an Appaloosa which seemed very familiar to Shaddrock. A figure appeared at the doorway of the farmhouse. The regulator recognized the outline of the man's Montana peak hat.

"¿Quien es Ud y que desear Ud?" Cougar demanded, holding the shotgun at his hip, the muzzles pointed upward. "Who are you and what do you want?" he repeated in English.

"You sound like an American, feller," Quint replied calmly, his hand resting on the grips of his Smith & Wesson. "Pretty good Spanish though."

"It'll do," the bounty hunter declared, stepping closer. "How many languages I gotta use before I get an answer to my question, feller?"

"Seein' as how I've got a dozen men surrounding this place with guns aimed at you, I figure you should be answerin' my questions first."

"You ain't asked any yet." Cougar grinned. "And I bet I can still take you apart with a load of buckshot even if your boys start puttin' lead in me."

"Tough man," Quint smiled thinly. "What's your name, feller?"

"Crowly," the bounty hunter lied smoothly. "Used to be Lieutenant Crowly when I rode with Jeb Stuart during the War for Southern Independence."

"War's been over awhile, mister," the gunfighter stated. "What the hell are you doin' out here?"

"Right now I'm holding a Greener twelve gauge

93

that could blow you and the four fellers with you to hell," Cougar answered. "If you wasn't an American, I'd guess the rest of these guys to be *bandidos.*"

"You ever hear of the Comancheros, Crowly?" Quint inquired.

"Sure," the regulator said with a nod, lowering his shotgun. "If you fellers plan to rob me, you picked one helluva poor choice for a victim."

He stepped closer and kicked a lump amid the shadows. The shape rolled over into a natural spotlight of moon beams. Fred Dearn's lifeless face stared up at the night sky. "Maybe you'll find something worth taking on him," Cougar told them. "There's two more inside. They're bounty hunters so they might have a dollar or two in their pockets."

"Bounty hunters?" Quint's eyebrows rose. "And what were *you* doing with them, Crowly?"

"I was busy killing them a minute ago." Cougar shrugged. "They captured me at my camp a few miles from here. Then they found somethin' that interested them a whole lot. One of the fellers said there was a big camp of outlaws up ahead. Must have been you fellers. I reckon Comancheros have a bounty on them."

"Nobody's gonna collect it," the gunfighter remarked flatly.

"Those three must've figured they could," Cougar replied. "They killed the *peones* that owned this little sheep farm and took over the place. Then they had a vote and decided I wasn't worth the trouble to guard. They were going to kill me, so I killed them."

"Just like that, huh?" Jethro Mackall snorted.

"No," the bounty hunter said. "But I managed."

"How come these regulators grabbed you, Crowly?" Shaddrock demanded, concealing his surprise at the fabricated story his partner had put together.

"Another *gringo,* eh?" the senior bounty hunter grinned. "Well, there's an eight hundred dollar price on my head in Texas. Guess they planned to haul me back to collect it."

"Is that a fact?" Quint inquired. "What did you do to earn this honor?"

"Last year I deserted from the Army," Cougar answered. "After the war, I decided to try to forget the past and joined up with the blue-bellies. That was a mistake. Hell, I was a commissioned officer in the Confederacy, but the cavalry told me I couldn't expect to receive any rank above sergeant because I'm a former Johnny Reb. Why, Jeb Stuart once told me I was the best weapons OIC in his outfit. He had me and my boys in charge of the Gatling guns—and we hardly ever had one jam up and when it did, my men could clear it quicker than you can curse General Sherman."

"That a fact?" the pistolman asked, surprise altering his hatchet face.

"Didn't matter none to those Yankee bastards," Cougar continued. "They made me a lousy private and gave me more shit than a herd of buffaloes can dump in a year. Finally, I had enough and I up and left—with a pretty good sized portion of an Army payroll I took from a couple of officers." He shrugged. "They didn't say I couldn't have it. 'Course, they were dead."

95

"You say you handled Gatlings," Quint inquired. "Did that include maintenance and repair?"

"Sure. Used to fix 'em with little more than a Bowie knife and spit."

"Ever handle the new models?"

"I've seen them, but I never fired one. The blue-bellies wouldn't even let me touch the ones they had. Hell, the principal construction is the same. I could'a learned in no time if I'd had the chance." The bounty hunter looked up at Quint. "If you fellers plan to kill me, can I at least have a drink before you do it?"

"We'll talk about that later," the pistolman said. "Right now, you put that shotgun on the ground and take off that gunbelt. We aren't going to kill you—at least not until Ramon Larson has a chance to decide if you'd be more useful alive."

"I don't trust him," Shaddrock remarked flatly.

Cougar glared at him.

"We don't trust *you* yet," Quint snapped. "The rest of us will decide if this feller joins us or not."

"So make your own mistakes." Shaddrock shrugged.

The senior bounty hunter surrendered his weapons to the Comancheros. Javier Gomez, another ex-*bandido,* and Miguel, the half-breed Yaqui, took the guns to Quint. The pistolman examined Cougar's gunbelt with interest.

"Real professional," he commented.

"I ain't exactly an amateur," the bounty hunter replied.

"One of those horses belong to you?"

"The Appaloosa stallion."

"Right fine animal." The gunfighter smiled. "Jethro, make sure he ain't got any weapons in the saddle bags on that critter."

"Shore 'nuff," the hillbilly said, swinging down from the pinto that had formerly belonged to Arlon Ford.

"Gomez, take some men and check inside the hut," Quint ordered. "Make sure this feller ain't tellin' us a bunch of windy."

"*Si, señor* Quint," the Mexican replied.

"I took their guns and stacked them inside," Cougar told the group of Comancheros that marched to the hut. "Don't any of you fellers have a little bottle of something with alcohol in it?"

Quint sneered. "You just hold your thirst until we get your ass to the camp, Crowly."

"Sure hope that won't be too long," Cougar replied, wiping the back of his hand across his mouth.

Delighted voices issued from the hut, accompanied by the sounds of fists striking flesh. The Comancheros emerged with Townsend McClean between them. They dragged the semiconscious regulator from the adobe house and threw him to the ground. One of the men kicked him in the ribs. McClean groaned and stirred weakly.

"This one is still alive," Gomez declared happily.

"Right now," Quint replied coldly, swinging down from his mount.

"We found these in the pockets of his coat, the Mexican added, holding up two crumpled reward posters. "The *bastardo is* a bounty hunter."

Jethro led the Appaloosa next to Shaddrock's

Morgan. Cougar climbed into the saddle. Shaddrock grinned at his partner. "You left one alive, Crowly," he said mockingly.

"Nobody's right all the time." The senior bounty hunter shrugged.

"What's your name, regulator?" Quint demanded.

McClean slowly rose to his feet. His eyes bulged in terror from his battered, bloodied face. His voice quivered as he answered the gunfighter.

"Most of these fellers have a price on their heads," Quint commented. "You wanta try to collect it now?"

"No, sir," McClean shook his head.

"You figure you'd like to go back with us and see what sort of reception you'll get as a guest in our camp?"

The regulator shook his head harder. "Listen, mister . . ."

"No, you listen, man hunter!" the gunfighter hissed. "Your breed are back-shootin' scum that ain't got the sand to face a man on equal terms."

"I gotta tell you somethin'," McClean began.

"Shut up!" Quint snapped. "You know how to use a pistol, don't you?"

"I . . ." McClean stepped back helplessly.

"Somebody throw this bastard a gun." The pistolman smiled, his hand dropping to the .44 Smith & Wesson on his hip.

"No!" the bounty hunter cried.

"Here, *cobarde!*" Miguel sneered, tossing his Whitney Colt to the regulator.

McClean instinctively caught the revolver in both hands.

"You've got a gun, feller," Wesley Quint declared coldly. "Use it."

"I'm tryin' to tell you . . ." McClean stammered, holding the Whitney to his chest like an amulet.

"You ain't got nothin' to tell us," the gunfighter declared flatly.

The other Comancheros moved away from the pair, walking or leading their horses from the range of fire. Shaddrock and Cougar followed the gang's example, urging their mounts several yards to the right. Two lanterns had been left near Quint and McClean to cast a harsh yellow light on the two men. The gunfighter's mouth curled up at the corners in a cruel grin, his fingers hovering close to the ivory grips of the Smith & Wesson. McClean's knuckles whitened as he gripped the Colt's frame tightly.

"This is the only chance you got, regulator," Quint warned. "If you throw that gun down, you'll wind up havin' every Apache, Yaqui, and *bandido* torture our boys can figure out—and we got some mighty mean fellers in our outfit."

McClean swallowed nervously, his body trembling as he glanced from side to side at the hostile faces of the Comancheros.

"But if you use that gun and you can beat me," Quint continued calmly, "then the rest of these fellers will let you go. Your decision. It'll be the last mistake you ever make—either way."

McClean suddenly extended his arm with the Whitney in his fist, aiming at the gunfighter as his thumb earred back the hammer. The Smith & Wesson roared. The regulator's body staggered backward like a drunkard from the impact of a .44 slug in the chest. Quint fired again. A second 200 grain bullet smashed into Townsend McClean's torso, drilling through his heart to blast a gory exit hole beneath his left shoulder blade. The tall regulator fell into the hut. His limp fingers released the unfired Colt as he slumped to the ground, smearing blood on the adobe wall.

"Ain't nothin' in the world worse than a goddamn bounty hunter," Quint snorted, breaking open his Smith & Wesson to replace the spent cartridges with fresh shells.

"Guess not," Cougar replied with a shrug.

NINE

The empty tequila and whiskey bottles burst into fragments of flying glass as a volley of rapid .44 caliber projectiles smashed into them. Bullet holes appeared in the empty kegs and crates beneath the targets, splintering wood and bowling over the lighter objects. Cougar stopped turning the crank of the Gatling gun and turned to Ramon Larson.

"Bueno, señor Crowly." The Comanchero leader smiled. The two men stood at the improvised firing range that had been set up beyond the rock formations to avoid the hazard of ricocheting rounds on stone walls. "You handle that weapon very well, indeed."

"Gracias, jefe," the bounty hunter replied. "So you think you can find a place for me among your *hombres?"*

"Sí." Larson nodded. "If you can repair a Gatling as well as you shoot one."

"I can," Cougar assured him.

"You better," the Comanchero warned. "I have many men that can fire a Gatling gun, but I need someone who can keep it firing."

"You got him," the regulator stated.

"We will see, Crowly," Larson said without any inflection in his voice to indicate his thoughts. "You are a skilled professional, you speak Spanish like a *mejicano,* and I think you are smarter than any two men I have with the exceptions of Quint, Alverez, and maybe the other *gringo* Shaddrock. I am suspicious of a gift such as you. God does not grant abundant favors to Comancheros. In fact, God does not even exist."

"How do you know?" Cougar inquired. "Did He tell you He doesn't?"

"I look at a world that is all *mierda*—shit—and I know," Larson replied bitterly. "I see men that are nothing but garbage and women that are whores."

"Maybe you're hanging around with the wrong crowd."

The Comanchero smiled. "You are a bold man, Crowly. I like that—but I don't like too much of it."

"I am also a thirsty man," Cougar replied. "There's still some whiskey or tequila around here, isn't there?"

"From what they told me, you should have had enough last night to keep you satisfied for a while, but I suppose we can spare another drink or two."

Shaddrock approached the pair. Like Cougar, his weapons had not been returned and he felt awkward unarmed. The younger bounty hunter could imagine how much more uncomfortable his partner felt since Cougar was even more accustomed to carrying an arsenal.

"Ah, the other new member of our family." Larson chuckled. "How are you this morning?"

"I've had worse hangovers, *jefe,*" Shaddrock

replied.

"So you have begun to learn some *espanol*, no?" the Comanchero said. "To call me "chief" is a good way to start. You might learn more words from Crowly here. He's a smart man, like you."

"He can't be too smart if he got himself captured by three bottom-of-the-barrel regulators," Shaddrock snorted, glancing contemptuously at Cougar. "Then he got falling down drunk last night."

"And I can still shoot your eyes out the next morning, feller," the senior bounty hunter replied coldly. "You see what I did with this Gatling?"

"You turned a handle like a goddamn organ grinder." Shaddrock shrugged. "Where's your monkey? Of course, you sort'a look like one anyway..."

"And you look like you still have most of your teeth," Cougar commented. "Don't know why you want to lose some now."

"Easy, *amigos*," Larson urged mockingly. "You two should not quarrel. You have much in common, no?"

"This guy and me don't have shit in common," Cougar answered angrily. "I heard about you, Shaddrock. A lousy card cheat who shot a feller when he caught you dealing from the bottom of the deck. Real impressive background."

"But his marksmanship yesterday was not to be scoffed at, Crowly," Larson stated. "He is very fast and very accurate with his *pistolas*. As I said, you two are much alike. You both use weapons well, you're both professionals when it comes to killing and"—the Comanchero grinned—"you're the only two men in my camp who I do not trust to carry arms."

103

"How long before I get my guns back?" Shaddrock inquired.

"That depends on how long it takes you to earn my trust." Larson shrugged. *"Both* of you."

He marched to a detail of Comancheros who'd stood guard over Cougar during the Gatling gun demonstration. Larson told the men to take the weapon back to the bivouac area while Shaddrock stepped closer to his partner.

"I thought you were supposed to remain on the outside so you could move in and help me if I needed it," he muttered.

"That's how we planned it," Cougar replied. "But we didn't know Colonel Sutton had hired three other bounty hunters to do the same job we were assigned to. The bastards caught me and figured out who I was. They were going to kill me so I didn't have any choice."

"That's what you get for being famous," Shaddrock commented. "At least I can use my real name."

"You're building a reputation," the senior bounty hunter assured him. "Later you'll wish you didn't have it."

"That was quite a story you came up with, *Crowly.*"

"Best I could come up with in a hurry," Cougar stated. "I ripped off my oak leaves from my tunic because too many folks know I was a major in the Confederate Army and still wear the rank. I figured maybe I could pass for a Gatling gun expert and Larson might decide I'd come in useful."

"You seem to know a lot about them."

"Actually, most of the Gatlings were manufactured

104

on the Union side during the war. The South had Doc Gatling but the North had the industrialization. Every one I used we'd taken from you Yankees."

"You seem to be convincing Larson. That's what counts," Shaddrock declared. "Why are you acting like you can't go half an hour without a drink?"

"Reckon these fellers will relax around me a little if they figure I'm a part-time drunkard. Larson already suspects we're too professional to just be falling into his lap by sheer chance, so we'd better not look *too* good for a while. Be careful around that character. He's a shrewd son of a bitch."

"I've noticed," Shaddrock assured him. "Have you got any ideas about what we're going to do now?"

"Not exactly," Cougar admitted. "But we'd better not act too chummy too fast. Let's both look around and learn what we can about the Comancheros and their camp. Then we'll try to discuss it when we get the chance."

But such an opportunity did not occur for the next three days. The regulators were put in separate tents that served as billets for the Comancheros. Larson's men watched the newcomers closely. They observed the bounty hunters' actions and occasionally conversed with them in an effort to catch any verbal slips that might prove either man to be other than he appeared. However, both men had selected cover stories they could uphold convincingly and the identities they'd assumed were close enough to their own personalities to assist in the charade.

Still, neither Shaddrock nor Cougar were permitted to leave the camp or carry weapons. The senior bounty hunter's expertise with Gatlings had him spending most of the daylight hours tending to the guns and their ammunition, but an armed guard always watched him at such times.

Shaddrock, however, received the most unsavory chores in the camp—assisting the cook, digging latrine ditches, and shoveling horse dung. At night, the younger man gratefully fell into his cot and slept soundly, despite the dangers of his environment and the noise of the hard-drinking, half-civilized Comancheros. Cougar continued to play his role as an alcoholic. He was never without a bottle—although he actually drank very little—and he'd stagger from the campfire to his tent in the evenings, much to the amusement of the gang members.

On the afternoon of the third day, Ramon Larson and twenty Comancheros mounted their horses and rode from the campsite, leaving Wesley Quint in command. Shaddrock and Cougar watched the riders vanish into the distance, a cloud of dust lingering in their wake.

"Where are they going?" Shaddrock asked Quint.

"Business trip," the gunfighter replied gruffly. His attitude toward the newcomer had become steadily more surly. "If Ramon figured it was any of *your* business, he would have told you."

"About how long will he be gone?" Cougar inquired, pulling a small bottle from his pocket and removing the cork.

"A couple days maybe," Quint said, sneering at the bounty hunter. Since he abstained from liquor because it might affect his reflexes, the pistolman regarded "Crowly's" drinking habits with utter contempt. "He'll probably bring back plenty of whiskey, so you'll have lots of reason to look forward to his return, won't you?"

"Reckon so," Cougar agreed, raising the redeye to his lips. He didn't open his mouth or swallow.

"A card cheat and a drunken Johnny Reb has-been." Quint scowled. "Pretty sorry Comanchero material we're getting these days."

He arrogantly swaggered to the center of camp. Shaddrock consulted his goldplated, turnip-shaped pocket watch as Cougar put the cork in his bottle and put it away.

"Camp'll be about half strength for a while," the senior bounty hunter remarked. "Considering all the drinking and crap these boys do, they should be mighty distracted."

"Four o'clock," Shaddrock announced, closing his watch. "Sun'll be setting in a couple hours and the fiesta starts. Figure we'll get a chance to talk?"

"After the party's going full steam," Cougar replied, walking to the campsite.

"Maybe we'll do a little bobbing for Gatlings," the younger man commented dryly.

The Comancheros followed their standard custom of steady consumption of tequila (the half-empty bottle of whiskey Cougar had was all that remained in the camp), tacos, chili, and whores. The arguments that became fist or knife fights were settled by the burly Luis. Drunken singing and boasting filled the night as usual.

107

With almost half of the outlaws gone, Shaddrock had to wash fewer pots, plates, and utensils. The cook, a fat, good-natured man named Enrique, told Shaddrock to leave the larger kettles and caldrons used to prepare chili and boil goat meat.

"We will let them soak tonight, no?" Enrique smiled. "Enjoy yourself tonight, American."

"Gracias, amigo," Shaddrock replied, wondering how a man like Enrique ever joined a gang of cutthroats like Larson's gang. He would have been startled to learn the cook had murdered his own children after his wife left him. The outcast killer never discussed his crime and few of the Comancheros were aware of Enrique's past.

The bounty hunter moved to a keg of alkali-laced desert water and turned on the tap to fill a basin. He stripped off his shirt and washed his lean, hard torso with a cloth and lye soap. Shaddrock had managed to survive four years in the thick of battle during the War Between the States without acquiring a scratch, but a star-shaped scar on his upper left arm told of the hazards of his current profession. A bullet had punched clean through the limb, luckily causing no lasting damage. Shaddrock might not be so fortunate the next time.

"My, my," a feminine voice remarked. "Look at what we've got here."

He turned to see Marie standing nearby. She openly appraised his bare chest with appreciation. Shaddrock wrung out the cloth and rinsed himself with fresh water from the keg.

"Just me, ma'am," he replied. "We've already

108

met."

"Sir Alexander—our resident knight."

"You remember."

"You sort of like Sir Galahad?" she asked, stepping closer.

"More like Lancelot," Shaddrock stated.

"Wasn't he the one who was fucking Guenevere?" Marie asked flatly.

The bounty hunter looked at her with surprise. "You got a real way with words, lady."

She laughed bitterly. "I thought you had me figured out, Alex."

"Not really," he admitted, toweling himself dry. "Although you do seem out of place here."

"I'm a former New Orleans whore," Marie answered. "Used to make a lot of money at it too. Made most of it lying on my back, but sometimes I earned a few dollars by taking the wallets of drunken customers."

"Did the latter foul up the former?"

"You guessed it." She shrugged. "A feller caught me stealing his cash and nearly beat me to death before I got to my Pepperbox pistol and put enough bullets in him to make him stop—for good."

"Self-defense."

"Bullshit," Marie snorted. "I would have gone to prison for life if they'd caught me. So I ran to little Ramon. He'd been one of my customers in the past. Not as bad as some men I've known. Ramon doesn't beat me or go for sick little bedroom games." She sighed. "Of course, since he can hardly get it up, he can't be too fancy with it."

"I thought he was supposed to be the greatest lover in the Western Hemisphere."

She chuckled. "Ramon's ego is a lot bigger than his pecker. It's all an act, just like him pretending he's a pirate with that silly sword of his. Ramon is full of shit. Let him play his games and he's happy."

"And you're his woman."

"It doesn't do me much good," she replied. "Still, I don't have to be in that tent with those five sows, getting screwed by this bunch of scum. But a woman needs a man once in a while. A *real* man."

"Makes sense," Shaddrock agreed, pulling on his shirt. "Since a man needs a woman from time to time too. I guess that's natural."

"You feeling a need now?" Marie inquired, running her pink tongue along her ripe lower lip.

"For a *real* woman," he said with a nod.

"One'll be waiting for you in King Arthur's tent, Lancelot," she assured him.

Marie turned and walked away.

Half an hour later, Shaddrock entered the private quarters of Ramon Larson. A single candle illuminated the interior of the tent. The Comanchero had supplied himself with plenty of creature comforts—a chest of drawers, a full-length mirror, a rolltop desk, a hand-carved table with chairs, and a four poster bed. Marie waited for him, lying on the mattress with a white linen sheet drawn up to her breasts.

"While the king's away, the queen will play, huh?" he remarked, removing his Stetson.

"The night chill still bothers me, Alex," she told him as she drew back the sheet. "And I don't want te-

110

quila or a horse blanket to warm me."

The bounty hunter gazed down at her naked body. She was even more beautiful than he'd imagined. Marie's firm globular breasts were capped by erect brown nipples. The curves of her torso flowed smoothly into a narrow waist and flared at the hips before meeting her long creamy thighs and tapered legs. Marie slowly spread her lower limbs to display the triangle of dark red hair. She inserted two fingers and methodically worked her hand back and forth.

"You don't look so cold to me, lady," Shaddrock commented, holding his hat at chest level. With a twist of the wrist, he hurled the Stetson. It sailed quickly past the candle, creating a current of air that extinguished the flame.

"Your aim as good with other things besides pistols and headgear?" Marie's voice inquired from the darkness.

"You'll find out in a minute," he replied, approaching the bed.

He sat on the corner of the mattress and began to unbutton his shirt. Marie rose to meet him, her hand slipping inside his clothes to caress his chest as their mouths crushed together. Tongues probed eagerly. Shaddrock's fingers found her breasts, fondling gently, teasing the nipples with his skilled touch.

Marie unbuttoned his trousers and stroked his erect manhood. Her body shifted forward and her lips assumed the task, drawing his stiff member into her mouth with slow deliberate care. Shaddrock's hand found her love center and stimulated her in turn. The tempo of their caresses increased gradually until his arm jerked to and fro rapidly and her head bobbed up and down, long scarlet locks cascading on his thighs.

At last he exploded his load. Marie lay back and moaned happily while Shaddrock's fingers continued to bring her to a climax. He straddled the woman, lowering his mouth to her breasts, kissing and sucking tenderly. Marie quivered violently, her nails raking his back before she gasped in ecstasy.

"Not a bad warmup," she whispered. "But I hope you aren't all done in."

"Don't worry, lady," Shaddrock assured her. "There's lots more to come."

Two hours later, the bounty hunter cautiously emerged from the tent, fully clothed. Inside, Marie snored contentedly. Shaddrock smiled. That was a night he'd never forget and he wagered she'd remember the knight as well. As he strolled across the camp with his hands in his pockets, the regulator wondered how long Larson would be away.

"I hope you got that out of your system."

Shaddrock turned sharply, startled by the unexpected voice behind him. The light of the campfire revealed enough of Cougar's face to allow his partner to see an expression of irritation. The senior bounty hunter shook his head.

"One of these days your pecker is gonna get you killed," he rasped.

"Is there a better way?" Shaddrock replied mildly.

"Screwing Ramon Larson's mistress, for crissake," Cougar muttered. "Better hope these guys didn't see you go in there."

"How'd you know where I was?"

"I know *you*," Cougar snorted. "I could guess the rest. Come on."

He led Shaddrock to a group of boulders. A sentry sat cross-legged on the ground, his head bowed forward in slumber. Shaddrock glanced down at him and turned to his partner with surprise.

"Don't worry," Cougar assured him. "This feller ain't in any condition to hear a word we say."

Shaddrock noticed an empty tequila bottle lying beside the man. Next to it was a metal dish with some shredded brown leaves and rolling papers. The bounty hunter's nose recoiled at the sickly sweet scent that dominated the area.

"He's been sitting here drinking liquor and smoking marijuana cigarettes for hours," Cougar explained. "This feller couldn't tell you what his name is let alone pay any attention to us."

"Is that smell from his tobacco?" Shaddrock asked.

"Marijuana ain't tobacco," the senior hunter replied. "It's a whoopie weed. Sort'a works like alcohol except it mellows a feller out more and you don't have a hangover later."

"You don't go crazy or anything like that?" Shaddrock wondered, kneeling by the intoxicated Comanchero.

"Just the opposite," Cougar answered.

"Think I'll try a little of this stuff," the younger hunter said, plucking at the leaves. "Why's he keep it in a little pot?"

Cougar ignored the question. "We've got to figure out how to take advantage of Larson's absence to

113

get the guns."

"What's this green shit?"

"He must've got a little grass mixed into it."

Shaddrock sprinkled some marijuana on a paper, then rolled and licked it down. "What do you suggest we do?"

"First of all . . ."

"Got a match?"

"Hell," Cougar groaned, striking a Lucifer on his thumb nail. Shaddrock inserted the cigarette into the flame and puffed. He inhaled deeply and immediately coughed, nearly choking.

"I don't usually smoke, you know," Shaddrock gasped.

"You pick a helluva time to do it." Cougar sighed. "First of all, not all of the Comancheros will be like this feller." He pointed at the unconscious man at their feet. "We'll have to kill 'em anyway we can. Bare hands, rocks, whatever. Then we take their weapons."

Shaddrock's cheeks deflated as he sucked on the marijuana.

"Quint is the most dangerous man here. He has a reputation for being one of the fastest guns in the Southwest and we saw how he got it. McClean wasn't any pistolman, but he still had a gun in his hand when Quint drew on him."

Shaddrock nodded, then tilted back his head and allowed the smoke to drift from his nostrils.

"Alverez went with Larson, so we don't have much to worry about in a battle of wits. Luis is a tough bastard, but he's all muscle. Mackall is about as smart, but they're still plenty mean and hard. The others aren't exactly choirboys. They might not know how to write their own names, but they're still handy with a gun or a knife, despite all the drinking and screwing around they do."

"Yeah," Shaddrock agreed, closing his eyes as he drew on the cigarette.

"We'll take out the guards and Quint and maybe a couple of others. Then we get the Gatlings and deal with the rest."

"Sounds good." The younger bounty hunter smiled.

"You ever handle a Gatling?"

"Huh?" Shaddrock stared at Cougar with a blank expression.

"Oh, hell," Cougar muttered sourly. "You aren't in any shape to do anything tonight."

"Sure I am," Shaddrock insisted with a stupid grin. "Now, what were we talking about?"

"Never mind," the senior bounty hunter sighed. "We'll discuss it tomorrow."

TEN

The morning destroyed Cougar's plan as Ramon Larson and his twenty men returned shortly after the break of dawn. The Comanchero leader swung down from the back of his handsome white Arabian and marched angrily into the heart of the camp. Wesley Quint barely glanced at him as the gunfighter laboriously shaved with a small mirror and a dull razor.

"Where the hell are the sentries, Quint?" Larson demanded.

"Didn't post any this morning," the pistolman replied, turning to his commander. The lather on his face reduced the axe-blade quality of his features, yet his eyes remained as hard as tempered steel. "Most of those damn fools got drunk last night and woke up sicker than an old dog. I put a couple of fellers on the rocks. One fell asleep and the other started pukin' so bad he fell and damn near broke a leg. So I told them to forget it today."

"You did what?" the Comanchero boss glared at him. "That's not like you, Quint. What do you think you're doing?"

"*You* told me not to ride these fellers with spurs on. You told me to let them have their tequila and whores and not to make a federal case outta their behavior."

116

Quint smiled maliciously. "That's what I done and you can see what a bunch of shit-for-brains morons you got working for you."

"And I'm looking at one of them!"

The gunfighter's eyes narrowed and his knife-slash mouth formed a line as hard as the barrel of a sixgun. "Don't bad-mouth me, Ramon. I ain't one of your *peones.*"

"Then why did you do this *stupido* thing?" Larson replied.

"I've tried to tell you these men need more discipline and less liquor and women. Maybe now you'll listen to me."

"Damn it, Quint! I leave the camp for one day and you ruin our security to make a point! *Cristo!* I've set up the first Gatling gun sale with a band of Kiowas that want to go on the warpath against the pony soldiers. I'm going to need some reliable men in case those *Indio* savages decided to make trouble—to say nothing of the *gringo* Army!"

"You've still got those guys," Quint declared, pointing at the Comancheros who'd returned with Larson.

"Si." The outlaw leader nodded. "But I don't want this camp unguarded. I'll have to leave some of them here. I also want two competent men with the Gatling guns. Where's Crowly?"

"I thought you wanted a *competent* man," the gunfighter sneered.

"I don't care if Crowly lives in a fucking bottle," Larson snapped. "He still handles a Gatling better than anyone we've got and he knows what to do if one jams or misfires."

"He's around someplace—probably sitting on his ass drunk."

"If he's able to ride, he goes with us. How many others are in fighting condition?"

"Luis, of course," Quint replied. "That big bastard is always alert and eager to bust heads. Mackall's in pretty fair shape. Ruiz, Martinez, and a couple of others seem to be able to function without throwing up."

"What about Shaddrock?"

"Enrique's got him scrubbing the breakfast plates. Not many of these fellers felt like eating, so I guess he'll be done by now. He seemed fit enough, I reckon."

"Tell him to get his horse saddled. Get your own ready too. I'm putting Alverez in charge of the camp. When we get back, I expect to find it secure—something *you* failed to manage!"

"Hell, I'd rather ride into a little action than play wet nurse to these scum anyway." Quint shrugged.

Larson didn't make a comment. The pistolman's ability with a sixgun bordered on magic and the Comancheros would need all the hot-lead witchcraft they could muster if they encountered trouble in Texas.

Twenty-one Comancheros, including Shaddrock and Cougar, crossed the border that afternoon. Most wore dirty white *peone* clothing and straw *sombreros.* Larson and a few others had donned more colorful *vaquero* garments and rode at the head of the congregation. A Conestoga wagon rolled slowly among the *"peones."*

The bounty hunters' weapons had not been returned, but Cougar had been instructed to ride near the wagon in case they needed the Gatling guns inside the vehicle. Larson assured Shaddrock he'd be given a carbine if any shooting occurred. Neither man found much comfort in these conditions.

The riders traveled through arid Texas plains, surrounded by cactus, sagebrush, and sand dunes. Prairie dogs scrambled for their holes and jackrabbits bounded for cover as the Comancheros approached. Above them, in the distance, three buzzards circled patiently in the brilliant blue sky. Several Comancheros superstitiously feared the birds were a bad omen and crossed themselves. Cougar smiled. He felt no repulsion toward the scavengers and admired their grace, finding beauty in creatures most regard with utter loathing. The vultures served a valid natural function. Of course, the bounty hunter did not view death with dread. To Cougar, it was the ultimate destination at the end of a long hard ride which everyone must make.

Shaddrock failed to notice the birds.

Then a column of Indians appeared at the summit of a sand dune. Unshod hooves silently trod the sand as the Kiowas urged their ponies forward. Another column followed, moving in a regimented, disciplined manner that would have done justice to a crack cavalry regiment. A third line of braves rose behind them.

Forty-six Indians dressed in buckskin, feathers, and war paint slowly approached the Comancheros. A few carried bows and lances, but most had acquired firearms from raids on white settlers and from unprincipled gunrunners like Larson. The majority of their weapons were muzzle-loaders or single-shot breech-loaders. However, more than one brave had a Spencer or Henry repeater.

"Well, Shaddrock," Ramon Larson began, turning to the bounty hunter who rode to the left of the Comanchero boss and wore a *vaquero* silk shirt, chaps, and low crown hat because he happened to be the only man tall and lean enough to fit the clothing. "What do you think of our customers?"

"I think they'd better want to do business peaceably or we've got a helluva problem on our hands," Shaddrock replied flatly.

"Relax," Larson assured him. "I've done business with Black Eagle and his men before. Like all *Indios,* they're *stupido* savages. Black Eagle thinks he can wear down your *gringo* Army with his little band and drive them out of Kiowa territory. He hates *Anglos* and *Mejicanos,* but he has enough sense to realize he needs men like me to get guns and liquor. If he killed me, he'd lose a valuable source of supplies. Besides, we're better armed than his men."

"But there's a lot more of them," the bounty hunter remarked.

"Scared, Shaddrock?" Quint mockingly asked.

"I'd feel more secure if I had a gun," Shaddrock admitted.

"You'll get a gun if you need one," the pistolman assured him.

"Besides," Larson added. "That is why we brought *two* Gatlings. The empty one we sell and the loaded gun is ready in case our buyers do not wish

120

to be agreeable."

A stocky brave on the blanket-clad back of a piebald mustang drew closer. His broad, paint-streaked face seemed to be carved of copper-brown granite. The modified warbonnet of a sub-chief adorned his head. Ramon Larson flamboyantly bowed at the Indian.

"Buenos dios, Black Eagle," he greeted. "I trust you brought the gold you promised, no?"

"I have yellow metal," the Indian replied gruffly. "You have gun that shoots with many voices?"

"Si, amigo." The Comanchero smiled. "I would not disappoint a valued customer like you."

"I feel more trust if you not ride with a white eyes on each side of you," Black Eagle stated grimly.

Quint's hand draped the butt of his holstered Smith & Wesson.

"Have you killed many pony soldiers, Black Eagle?" Shaddrock asked in a conversational tone.

"Not many," the Kiowa confessed stiffly.

"I have." The bounty hunter grinned. "And it's alright with me if you kill all the ones I missed."

The corners of Black Eagle's mouth curled up slightly. "I see gun now."

"Follow us, *amigo,"* Larson told him. He leaned toward Shaddrock as he pulled the reins of his mount to turn the animal around. "Good work," he whispered. "You think fast."

Cougar, dressed in faded white *peone* garb and a battered *sombrero,* assisted four Comancheros as they hauled one of the Gatlings from the back of the Conestoga. The heavy weapon was awkward due to its size and shape, but it was mounted on a platform with wheels and thus easily moved once placed on the ground. Black Eagle dismounted and examined the Gatling. Cougar suspected the Indian didn't have any idea how to operate or load the gun, but his pride made him pretend he knew all about it. The bounty hunter didn't volunteer any information. Neither did the Comancheros.

"How much ammunition do we get with gun?" the Kiowa asked.

"The ammunition is almost as difficult to acquire as the guns themselves," Larson explained. "This weapon fires cartridges, like your Henry carbine. This is not easy to get and we must charge you accordingly."

"Supply and demand," Shaddrock muttered, steering his Morgan near Cougar.

"Don't you believe in free enterprise?" his partner rasped.

Black Eagle barked a command in his guttural native tongue. A young brave drew a bulging leather pouch from a saddle bag and jogged forward. The Indian leader took the parfleche and handed it to Larson.

"There is gold," he declared flatly. "How much ammunition does it buy?"

The Comanchero poured part of the contents into his hand and examined it with a restrained smile. The nuggets were genuine and larger than most. The bag had too much gold to fit in a single palm. He handed the first fistful to Quint and inspected the rest.

"Five hundred rounds," Larson told Black Eagle.

The Indian's eyes widened. "That is many bullets," he said. Since he could not count to one hundred, he knew five times that number must be great indeed.

"Almost a thousand," the Comanchero said.

A thousand! Black Eagle's mouth fell open. White men spoke of thousands only when they discussed buffalo herds and fish in rivers and stars in the sky. It was too large an amount for him to comprehend. "You have deal, Larson," Black Eagle announced.

"Bueno," the Comanchero boss agreed. He turned to his men. "Unload five hundred rounds of ammunition for our *amigo,* Black Eagle."

As the outlaws followed their commander's orders, Shaddrock leaned to the right in his saddle to address Cougar. "How long will that many cartridges last?"

"That depends on how often they fire the gun," the bounty hunter replied simply. "That is: Assuming they can figure out how to load it in the first place. They'll probably manage after a while. Then they'll probably burn up lots of ammunition trying it out. If they get a little liquor in them, they might waste it all in one night."

"And they might still have enough left to kill a lot of American soldiers and settlers too," Shaddrock said grimly.

"Don't worry about that," Cougar assured him. "Even these modified Gatlings won't fire more than a couple hundred rounds without jamming or misfiring. Then these Kiowas will be stuck with a heavy piece of worthless junk on their hands. They would have done better to buy rifles or stick with bows and arrows. Black Eagle had just paid for something he doesn't have the technology to handle."

"Where'd you learn a fancy word like technology?"

"There's books about other sciences besides pugilism, Shaddrock." The senior man grinned.

"Aw, shut up," his partner rasped.

The Kiowas departed with their new toy and the congregation of Comancheros headed toward the border. Ramon Larson laughed aloud as he rode at the head of the formation. "May all my customers be *estuipdos* like Black Eagle!"

"Reckon that red-nigger give you about ten thousand in gold, Ramon," Quint remarked with a wry grin. "The dumb bastard didn't even test the Gatling before he bought it."

"He can test it later with the three hundred and fifty cartridges I sold him." Larson chuckled. "That *idiota* can hardly count without using his fingers. He'll never realize we gave him less than we promised or that he paid enough for all seven Gatlings!"

"Ten thousand dollars sounds about right," Shaddrock whispered sourly. One of the guns was now gone and that whittled away part of the bounty hunters' reward—if they ever managed to collect it.

"I'll be glad when we get back to the camp," the gunfighter commented, glancing about their bleak surroudings. Sand dunes loomed on both sides of the Comancheros. A single tree jutted from the brown-gray surface, its tiny, dead frame too gnarled and twisted to be recognizable.

"Si," Javier Gomez agreed. The former *bandido* wiped sweat from his bearded face with a handker-

124

chief as he rode behind Wesley Quint. "This desert is as lonely as death itself."

A .52 caliber bullet punched through the white silk in his hand and smashed into his left eyebrow. The impact hurled Gomez from his saddle. He was dead before he could hear the report of the Spencer carbine on the sand dune. His handkerchief lay beside his bloody faced corpse. A smashed red glob in the cloth had formerly been the Comanchero's eyeball before the slug popped it abruptly from a cracked socket.

More gunshots exploded from the dune and two Comancheros toppled to the ground. Blue-clad figures on horseback charged from the summit their descent less quiet and unformed than the Kiowas' had been, but much faster.

"Fuckin' soldiers!" Quint snarled, unnecessarilly identifying their assailants.

"Helluva time for the cavalry to arrive," Shaddrock muttered, hugging the neck of his Morgan as Spencer-born hail pelted the group.

There was nothing to use for cover and the Army patrol outnumbered the Comancheros almost three to one. Larson didn't have to yell *"vamanous"*. They had only one choice of action—run like hell.

Bullets sizzled like molten-lead rain around the Comancheros as they galloped for their lives. More projectiles struck flesh. A round tugged at the collar of Shaddrock's shirt, hissing like a demon serpent as it passed near his ear. Another slug plowed into Ramon Larson's Arabian stallion. The white steed whinnied in agony as the bullet punctured the side of its neck and ripped an exit wound in the animal's throat.

125

Larson cried out in alarm before he was hurled from the saddle, pitched head over heels when his mount unceremoniously collapsed.

Cougar rode close to the clattering Conestoga, drawing up to its opening at the rear. Sucking in a deep breath, he prayed he was close enough to the wagon and it wouldn't move out of reach. Kicking free of the stirrups, he hurled himself from the back of his Appaloosa and dove into the gap amid the canvas-draped Conestoga. As agile as the big cat that supplied his nickname, Cougar landed nimbly inside the wagon, yet his left forearm slammed into the frame of the Gatling gun.

"I'm getting too old for this shit," he muttered, rubbing his smarting limb.

A Spencer bullet splintered wood from one of the wagon's ribs over Cougar's head. *Damn it,* he thought. *Leave it to a bunch of assholes in Yankee blue to do something like this!* Shifting the Gatling toward the opening, Cougar crouched behind the gun. A dozen or more cavalry troops were closing in fast, weapons blazing. The bounty hunter didn't want to shoot any of the soldiers—unfortunately, the feeling wasn't mutual.

Pushing the bulk of the Gatling with his knee, he managed to point the multimuzzled barrels low and turned the crank. Bullets rattled from the big gun like a deranged woodpecker attacking an iron post. Sand spat near the hooves of the advancing horses. Cavalry mounts reared in terror, throwing uniformed riders from their backs. Occasionally a slug struck an animal's shin, smashing bone and sending horse and soldier tumbling to the ground.

Cougar moved the Gatling to avoid shooting fallen troops. The vibrating weapon threatened to jar his kneecap apart, but he kept firing low at the hooves of the cavalry patrol. He was grateful the Comancheros on horse back were in front of the wagon, unable to witness his efforts to spare the soldiers' lives.

Shaddrock was too busy to pay attention to his partner's activities. He'd seen Ramon Larson crash to the ground from his mortally wounded mount. At first, the regulator feared the Comanchero leader had broken his neck from the fall, but Larson laboriously crawled to his hands and knees and shook his head slowly.

"Stay where you are, you ten thousand dollar son of a bitch," the bounty hunter hissed through clenched teeth. "The goddamn Army's not going to get their hands on you until we can make the delivery!"

Galloping to the dazed Comanchero, Shaddrock pulled back on the reins and brought his horse to a snorting, unhappy halt. Swiftly, he swung down from the gelding and dashed to Larson's side. Seizing the gang leader by the back of the collar and belt, the bounty hunter hauled him upright. Thankful that Larson was small and slender, Shaddrock half threw the semiconscious man onto the back of his Morgan.

Spencer rounds kicked dirt near the regulator's feet, adding fear-powered adrenaline to his leap. He landed in the saddle, legs splayed, nearly knocking Larson off the horse in his haste. Shaddrock groaned when his crotch connected with the hard leather. Still, he managed to catch the Comanchero's shirtfront before Larson could topple once more to the ground.

"Hang on, damn it!" he snapped.

Larson nodded weakly, but his arms encircled Shaddrock's waist firmly as the bounty hunter urged his mount into a gallop.

Disoriented and startled by the rapid fire of the Gatling gun, the Army captain in charge of the patrol ordered his men to retreat—an unnecessary command since most of the soldiers were already fleeing for the safety of the sand dunes, many of them on foot. Larson's vision cleared as he gazed back at the results of the running gun battle. Numerous soldiers and horses lay sprawled on the ground.

"Cristo!" he exclaimed. "Whoever got to that Gatling, he has earned himself a fat bonus this day."

Shaddrock scanned the Comancheros, looking for Cougar. He recognized his partner's Appaloosa, his heart rising to his throat when he saw the saddle was vacant. The gang eased their horses to a halt and rapidly saw to the wounded members. Quint rode alongside Shaddrock's Morgan, leading the roan stallion that formerly belonged to the late Javier Gomez.

"You'll need a horse, Ramon," he stated.

"Si," the Comanchero leader agreed, dismounting from the back of the bounty hunter's beast. "But not as badly as I needed one a few minutes ago. *Gracias,* Shaddrock. You saved my life and I will not forget that."

"Uh-huh," Shaddrock replied absentmindedly, still searching the area in hopes of spotting Cougar.

"No offense, brave *amigo,"*—Larson grinned, climbing into the saddle of the roan—"but you are not the right sex for me to appreciate riding double with except in such emergencies, no?"

"Huh?" the regulator had failed to recognize the comment as a joke. "Oh, that's alright."

"Lucky those blue-bellies decided to haul ass," Cougar announced as he caught the reins of his Appaloosa. "That Gatling jammed up like a son of a bitch."

"Ah!" Larson declared brightly. "So our other new addition had proven himself this day. We are all fortunate you managed to get to the gun, Crowly. Needless to say, both of you are now Comancheros and you will be rewarded for your courage."

Shaddrock smiled widely, relieved to see his partner had not fallen victim to cavalry gunfire. *"Gracias, jefe,"* he replied.

"Por favor, amigo," the Comanchero urged. "Call me Ramon."

ELEVEN

Shaddrock and Cougar were treated as guests of honor at a banquet ordered by Ramon Larson. The camp cook, Enrique, prepared *carne de carnero* mutton instead of chili for the occasion. The bounty hunters' weapons were returned. Shaddrock smiled with pleasure as he donned his shoulder holsters rig and slid the Police Colts into leather. His partner buckled on his gunbelt with its Colt Dragoon and Bowie knife, a sigh of relief issuing from his lips. Even Shaddrock's derringer and brass knuckles were back in his possession.

Larson gave both men a bottle of red wine from a case he kept in his tent for special occasions. Marie wore a blue dress with lace frills at its long sleeves and high collar. The redheaded beauty hardly resembled a New Orleans whore in her dignified apparel and her scarlet hair arranged in a girlish ponytail. Most of the Comancheros joined in the spirit of the celebration. Jethro Mackall displayed his prowess with a bullwhip, lashing the flame from the wicks of candles. Luis, the Mexican giant, exhibited his incredible strength. Grinning with delight, Luis held an iron horseshoe in his big hands and twisted it like a strip of licorice.

Driven by his ego and strong drink, Larson joined in the show. He stepped to the center of the camp with a cantaloupe in his hand. The Comanchero boss tossed the melon into the air and reached for his cutlass. The excessive consumption of wine and tequila ruined his draw. The cantaloupe fell to earth before the blade cleared his sash. Several men snickered, but Larson picked up the melon and tried again. He missed. Comancheros laughed aloud and the embarrassed commander stubbornly repeated his failure a third time.

The cantaloupe rose into the air once more. This time spectators gasped as Ramon Larson lunged forward and thrust the tip of his cutlass neatly into the gourd. With a twist of the wrist, he flicked the cantaloupe off the blade and deftly slashed it in half.

"There, you *cabrons!*" he snarled in a slurred voice, his bleary eyes glaring at the Comancheros. "Laugh at Ramon Larson now!"

No one did. The outlaw chief stomped into his tent. Marie glanced longingly at Shaddrock, then followed Larson. The others accepted the fact the celebration had ended and shuffled to their billets and guard positions.

"Well, I guess we're adopted," Cougar told his partner as they watched the gang depart from the campfire.

"Yeah," Shaddrock agreed. "Feels good to be packing iron again. Any idea how it might help us get those Gatlings?"

"Not off hand," the senior bounty hunter admitted. "But I'm thinking on it."

131

"That just tickles me shitless," Shaddrock snorted sarcastically.

The following morning, Ramon Larson had an announcement that startled everyone in the camp—especially Shaddrock and Cougar.

"We're going to sell another Gatling gun, *companeros*," he declared, smiling at the surprised expressions that surrounded him. "This one is going to an old friend of mine . . . although Juan here, knows him far better than I."

Alverez looked up at the Comanchero leader with alarm on his face. "You speak of Tomas Montoya?"

"*Si.*" Larson chuckled. "Your former employer. I sent a messenger to Monterrey last month when I first thought of stealing the Gatlings. A contact man operates at the bullring there. The answer I received was: 'If you succeed at this *loco* scheme, I'll pay you seven thousand pesos for such a gun.' "

"But, Ramon," Alverez began. "If you send me to Monterrey, Montoya will kill me!"

Larson turned to Shaddrock and Cougar. "Juan was once Montoya's trusted lieutenant, until he decided to quit the *bandido* gang to go into business for himself. Tomas might have understood such ambition if Juan hadn't helped himself to a large portion of the band's loot and put a knife between the ribs of Montoya's younger brother."

"Ramon, you can't . . ." Alverez begged.

"*Callate!*" the Comanchero leader snapped. "Don't wet your trousers with fear, Juan. I plan to put my most trusted man in charge of this assignment. Since

132

you betrayed Tomas and you'd probably do the same to me if you had the *huevos* to do so, you don't qualify anyway."

"All right," Wesley Quint sighed. He sat on a nail keg, cleaning his Smith & Wesson with an oily rag and a barrel brush. "When do I leave?"

"The *hombre* who failed to post sentries for my camp while I was away thinks I would trust him with such a mission!" Larson laughed.

The gunfighter's hatchet face grew even more rigid with anger.

"No, neither of you will go to Monterrey." The Comanchero boss turned to the bounty hunters once more. "Instead, I will put my *amigo*, Shaddrock, in charge of the detail. The only man who has ever risked his life to save mine. Who could be better qualified?"

The regulator's face expressed his astonishment.

"Shit," Quint spat. "He don't even speak Mexican."

"And you speak very little and very poorly," Larson replied. "Unlike our other brave newcomer, *señor* Crowly. The man who had the presence of mind to use the Gatling on those *gringo* soldiers yesterday. A resourceful and courageous *hombre* as well as an excellent choice for translator, no?"

"Reckon we're really in the fold now," Cougar muttered to his partner.

"I just hope it doesn't fold *up* and crush us," Shaddrock rasped.

"You're saying you trust these *Anglos* more than you trust Quint and me?" Alverez demanded.

"I have reason, no?" Larson smiled. "But I don't

trust them *too* much. Luis?"

"*Si*, Ramon?" the huge Mexican replied quickly.

- "I want you and Gonzales, Orlando, Miguel and Santos to go along with our new-found friends. You will all take orders from them unless they try to steal the Gatling gun or keep the money for themselves."

"Then we kill them?" Luis grinned.

"How bright you've become." The Comanchero leader chuckled. "Now, let me tell you how you'll transport the Gatling, Shaddrock."

"Believe me, you've got my undivided attention," the bounty hunter assured him.

That afternoon, Shaddrock sat beside Cougar as the senior man held the reins of the two mule team that hauled the wagon loaded with two coffins. Larson's handpicked Comancheros accompanied the pair, riding on either side of them.

"You figure anybody's going to stop our little 'funeral' procession?" Shaddrock asked, tugging the brim of a straw sombrero over his eyes. He was glad a serape poncho covered his shoulder holsters, although he realized it would inhibit any attempt to draw the pistols.

"Not likely," Cougar replied. He was dressed in a similar outfit, but his serape was drawn over his right shoulder to allow access to the Colt Dragoon on his hip. "Unless somebody looks close and wonders why a *gringo* like you is riding with us or they catch too much Arkansas in my accent, I doubt if the *Federales* or the *rurales* will be curious enough to stop us."

"What's the difference between the two?"

"Federales are more or less the military police. *Rurales* are the provincial police. They're both plenty mean and pretty much do as they please, but the *rurales* tend to be easier to bribe."

"That's nice," Shaddrock mused. "What if they want to look inside those coffins?"

"Since they're supposed to contain my late wife, Elena, and my son, Jose, who were killed by Yaquis, I don't think that's likely. Hell, I'm taking my dead family to Monterrey so they can get a proper Catholic funeral. That oughta satisfy the authorities."

"What if it doesn't?"

"Then there'll be some *Federales* or *rurales* that'll be going to their own funerals."

"Larson gave us a mean crew alright," Shaddrock commented, glancing at their escort. "You figure we could take them?"

"Maybe," Cougar said in a flat voice. "But why take the risk? We've got one disassembled Gatling gun and no ammunition for it. Montoya must have his own cartridges. What good will it do if we blast these five guys? We still have about forty more to deal with before we can claim Larson and the rest of the guns."

"Guess we just play Comanchero for a while," Shaddrock sighed. "I just hope we can live long enough to take our bows after the curtain comes down."

"Worry about that when we get to the last act," Cougar advised.

By dusk they approached a small hamlet. The excited voices of the Comancheros suggested the place was not unknown to them. Luis steered his big sorrel close to the wagon.

"There is a cantina here," he announced. "Good tequila, mariachi music, pretty whores—not like the fat *putas* back at the camp. We stop here, no?"

"Pretty whores, you say?" Shaddrock inquired with interest.

"We're supposed to be a funeral procession," Cougar reminded them. "We'll look goddamn suspicious if a *rurale* patrol happens along and sees us having a celebration."

"We could tell them we're Irish," Shaddrock suggested. "Even Catholics have a wake on the Emerald Island."

"*Señor* Shaddrock is in charge, not you, Crowly," the big Mexican declared, his eyes narrowing. "You just follow orders and keep your mouth shut, *comprende?*"

Cougar shrugged, unwilling to get into a confrontation with Luis unless he had to.

"What do you say Shaddrock?" Miguel, the Yaqui half-breed inquired. "Do we visit the cantina or do you let this drunkard take command?"

"How pretty are these women?" the younger bounty hunter asked.

"Aw, hell," Cougar muttered.

Leaving the wagon, mules and horses at the local livery stable, the regulators and their Comanchero overseers headed for the cantina. There were no signs to declare the name of either the shabby tavern or the hamlet itself. If the men with Shaddrock and Cougar knew such information, they felt no need to share it. As they approached the cantina, gay mariachi music

136

hinted that the establishment had more to offer than its appearance suggested.

Inside, they discovered the cantina was handsomely equipped with good furniture, a large well-stocked bar, an enthusiastic if less than impressive group of troubadours, and a number of attractive young women clad in provocative dresses that offered a generous view of cleavage to the delight of the male patrons. Luis and the other Comancheros literally ran to the counter and demanded tequila. Cougar placed his shotgun on a table and sank into a chair, clucking his tongue with disgust. These morons were jeopardizing their mission, but the only way he could stop them would be to shoot the bastards. Shaddrock smiled at the prostitutes.

"Buenos noches, señoritas," he began, doffing his hat.

However, the Comancheros ignored such formalities and merely grabbed the nearest female and led them to the stairs. The outlaws whooped and laughed, stomping up the steps with their giggling playmates.

"You sure have a way with women, Shaddrock," the senior bounty hunter commented.

"I've never seen any evidence that you do that well with them," Shaddrock snorted, slumping into the chair across from his partner.

"I did once," Cougar replied simply. "That was enough."

The younger man saw the distant glaze of memories in Cougar's dark eyes. The legendary Cougar—indestructible, cunning, coldblooded, and totally ruthless—had never recovered from one injury. The death of his wife had hurt him so deeply, no other woman had fired any desire within him since. None of them could compete with the Lydia Cruthers he carried inside his broken heart.

Shaddrock wondered if he could ever love someone that much. He wasn't certain he'd want to. Yet, the relationship Cougar had with Lydia must have been very special, unlike anything the younger man had ever known. Should he pity his partner for his loss or envy him for what he'd had?

"Yeah," he replied because he didn't know anything else to say.

Cougar took a cigar from his pocket. "We'll have to be more careful than ever when we get back to the camp."

"I thought we'd become Larson's overnight favorites," Shaddrock said.

"That's what I mean," the older man answered, scratching a match on the table. "Larson belittled Quint and Alverez in front of the rest of his men and he praised us. That means we've got a couple of enemies back there."

The other bounty hunter nodded. "I've thought about that. Larson might have offended them enough to get a bullet or a knife blade for his remarks. He ought to know better than to insult his lieutenants that way."

Cougar lit his stogie. "His mind is slipping. Larson's actions are getting irrational. He's been around cutthroats so long he doesn't think he can trust anyone—including men who've proven themselves to be loyal."

"But he trusts us?"

"Does he?" Cougar smiled. "Don't forget Luis and the others are supposed to keep an eye on us."

"Yeah," Shaddrock agreed. "I see your point."

"Well, I see two handsome strangers from north of the border have decided to pay us a visit," a musical feminine voice announced in splendid English.

The bounty hunters turned to see a shapely young woman dressed in a blouse and ornate full skirt. Her long black hair framed a dark oval face. Sensuous lips parted in a suggestive smile and her eyes scanned the pair with hungry interest. Shaddrock grinned in return.

"You are lonely, *señor?*" she inquired. "Perhaps Sofia can give you some companionship, no?"

"Maybe she can, *yes,*" he replied. "Assuming you're Sofia."

She laughed lightly. "What about your friend? Doesn't he want a woman too?"

"I'm trying to cut down," Cougar told her.

Shaddrock and Sofia mounted the stairs, arm in arm. Moving down the narrow corridor, they reached the door with the numeral 2 painted on the top panel. She opened it and led the bounty hunter into the room.

"Do you have any preferences, *señor?*" Sofia inquired.

He looked at the massive brass framed bed in the center of the room and smiled. "Why don't we just lie down for a while and see what happens?"

"I know what will happen," the girl replied. "It's just a question of how."

Shaddrock tossed his sombrero onto a nearby chair and slipped off his serape while Sofia unbuttoned her blouse. He watched her strip with an appreciative eye, noting the fullness of her firm brown breasts and sturdy, erect nipples. Unbuckling his shoulder holsters, the bounty hunter shrugged out of the harness

139

as Sofia slid off her skirt.

Naked, the girl sprawled on the mattress, propping a hand under her chin. Shaddrock sat on the edge of the bed to pull off his boots. She ran a hand over his back, clad in longjohns, tracing the nails along his spine.

"Hurry, darling," Sofia whispered. "I grow impatient."

"I'm worth the wait," he assured her, standing to remove his trousers.

"Ah!" she smiled, staring at the bulge at the crotch of his drawers. "I believe you are."

"Seeing is believing," he replied.

Suddenly, the door burst open. A burly, black-bearded figure stormed into the room. He wore a dusty tan uniform, an officer's insignia on his shoulders, and a battered sombrero on his shaggy head. A Colt .44 revolver filled his fist.

"Roberto!" the girl exclaimed. "I thought you and your patrol had gone to Piedras Negras!"

"Callate!" he snarled, swinging the gun at Shaddrock as he cocked the hammer. "I should sew your *cullo* up, you *puta!"*

"I get the impression this is a family quarrel," Shaddrock commented with a nervous smile, gazing at the muzzle of the Colt as he stood in his underwear. "Maybe I'd better go."

"My husband is very angry with me," Sofia told him.

"I sorta guessed that," the bounty hunter stated. "But he's still pointing that gun at *me.*"

"Si. He sometimes kills my customers because he doesn't like it when I return to the profession that first attracted him to me. It is foolish, no?"

140

"Some folks got strange notions," the regulator agreed.

Quickly, he scooped up the pillow from the bed and hurled it at the jealous husband. Roberto's revolver roared and a bullet slashed through the pillowcase, showering the room with feathers. Still, the tactic served to distract the gunman and Shaddrock took advantage of it. He launched himself into Roberto. Both men fell back into the doorframe.

"Don't hurt him!" Sofia cried, not specifying who she was concerned about.

Shaddrock seized the wrist behind the revolver and twisted, forcing the finger open. The gun struck the floor as the angry Mexican grabbed his opponent's hair with his free hand. With a vicious jerk, he pulled back the bounty hunter's head and slammed a solid punch to his jaw that sent Shaddrock reeling into the corridor.

The American's back met the banister as Roberto followed him into the hallway. A fist whipped into Shaddrock's narrow midriff. The bounty hunter gasped. Then his adversary seized his throat with both hands and shoved hard, trying to strangle and hurl him over the railing simultaneously.

Lights burst before his eyes as consciousness began to fade from the regulator. Shaddrock didn't waste time trying to pry the strong grip from his neck. He folded a knee and rammed it into the man's ribcage forcibly. Roberto grunted. Shaddrock hit him again and both men staggered away from the rail.

"Gringo bastardo!" Roberto hissed, his bearded face scant inches from Shaddrock's as his hands continued to throttle the American.

The bounty hunter bent an elbow and slammed it

into the side of the Mexican's head. Roberto's grip weakened. The back of Shaddrock's fist caught him flush in the face. The fingers fell from the American's throat. A quick left hook knocked Roberto four steps backward.

With a snarl of fury, Roberto lunged at Shaddrock, hands once again flying for the bounty hunter's neck. Shaddrock let him close in, then clasped his hands together and thrust them between the assailant's arms. Roberto's hands clutched air an instant before the bounty hunter's fists smashed into the side of his jaw. The blow sent the Mexican hurtling into the banister. Wood cracked and broke away under the impact. Roberto screamed once as he plunged over the edge, fell to the landing below and tumbled gracelessly down the stairwell.

"Capitan!" a startled voice shouted from below.

Shaddrock gazed downstairs and saw six men in uniforms and sombreros similar to Roberto's, staring up at him. All of them held rifles—three were aimed at the bounty hunter.

TWELVE

"Shit," Cougar muttered, sliding his chair from the table.

He'd watched the *rurales* enter the cantina and hoped the provincial police had only come to the establishment as patrons and not to question anyone about the coffins in the wagon at the livery stable. The captain in charge of the patrol asked the fat-faced bartender if he'd seen his wife. The man shook his head, but his frightened glances toward the stairs betrayed his lie. Furious, the officer drew his revolver and headed for the steps. Cougar guessed there'd be trouble and, unfortunately, he was right.

The sawed-off Greener bellowed before the *rurale* troopers could open fire on Shaddrock. A blast of buckshot splattered one *rurale* tan tunic into bloody shreds, the impact hurtling the man across the room. Stray pellets bore into the upper arm and shoulder of another soldier, throwing him into an awkward shuffle until he connected with a nearby table and tipped it over as he fell to the floor.

Shaddrock took advantage of the distraction to retreat from the head of the stairs. A rifle discharged, its lead missile splintering wood from the broken railing. Sofia stood at the threshold of her bedroom, her

143

face buried in her hands.

"You killed him!" she wailed. "You killed Roberto!"

"If he isn't dead I'll give him a needle and thread if he still wants to use it," Shaddrock growled, pushing her aside as he rushed into the room to reclaim his Colts.

Cougar's shotgun roared again. Twelve gauge death shattered another *rurale's* face, nearly decapitating him. The bloodied trooper was pitched into his disoriented comrades as they swung their weapons toward the senior bounty hunter. Discarding his empty Greener as he ran, Cougar bolted to the bar and vaulted the counter. Bullets smashed into the framework and exploded tequila bottles behind the bar.

"Madre de Dios!" the bartender cried, fleeing from his station as fast as he could waddle.

Heavy footfalls and excited voices above told Cougar the Comancheros had been alerted by the gunshots. A pistol cracked from the stairwell and the jawbone of a *rurale* private burst in a shower of blood and dislodged teeth. The young Mexican wilted to the floor as the only trooper untouched by the gun battle darted away from the stairs, firing a hasty round at the unseen pistolman.

Peering around the corner of the bar, Cougar followed the *rurale's* progress, watching him through the sights of his Colt Dragoon. The big revolver snarled, drilling a .44 caliber lead ball into the trooper's midsection. The *rurale* doubled up with a strangled moan, dropping his rifle to clutch his wounded belly. Cougar put another bullet in the side

144

of the man's head and transformed his skull into a ghastly debris of bone and brain fragments.

The *rurale* with the buckshot ravaged arm rose unsteadily to his feet, leaning on his rifle like an old man with a cane. Clad only in chino trousers, Miguel appeared on the stairwell with a smoking Remington revolver in one hand and a bone-handled knife in the other. The half-breed's face twisted into a satanic mask as he shoved the gun into his waist band. Miguel gripped the knife by its tip and threw it. Before the dazed *rurale* could react, the weapon whistled through the air and the blade slammed into his chest like the beak of a metallic bird of prey.

The rurale shrieked in agony and stumbled back into a chair. He sat down hard, head tilted forward as though in slumber. The shaft of the knife protruded from his bloodied tunic like a grotesque decoration.

Cougar emerged from behind the bar, cautiously watching the prone bodies of the *rurale* patrol in case any of them retained enough life to pose any threat. Miguel bounded down the steps, followed by the other Comancheros. The senior bounty hunter moved to the door, concerned that more *rurales* might be lurking outside. Seven horses tied to the hitching rail assured him they'd dealt with the entire patrol.

"Roberto!" Sofia cried, descending the stairs—still naked as a plucked jaybird. "Forgive me, Roberto!"

"Isn't true love wonderful?" Shaddrock muttered. Clad in his longjohns, he would have been a ridiculous figure if he didn't have a Police Colt in each fist.

"And isn't fucking the wife of a rurale captain stupid," Cougar rasped as he retrieved his shotgun.

145

"How was I supposed to know that?" the younger bounty hunter demanded.

"Never mind," the other regulator replied. "You fellers better get dressed and ready to move. The party is officially over."

"Giving orders again, Crowly?" Luis asked coldly. Dressed only in longjohn drawers, his muscular frame appeared more formidable than ever. Thick black hair covered his massive chest and forearms, but the enormous biceps and triceps bulged beneath dark tan skin like the coils of a boa constrictor. The .52 caliber Spencer in his hands contributed to his quality of menece.

"Crowly's right," Shaddrock declared. "Get your gear and let's move."

The Comancheros growled with disgust, but they headed for the stairs, stepping over and around the *rurale* captain at the bottom. Sofia knelt by her husband, hugging his head to her large, firm breasts as she wept. Cougar shook his head slowly when the last man reached the top floor.

"Your command sure ain't off to a great start, Shaddrock." The senior bounty hunter chuckled.

"At least we didn't lose any men," his partner replied with a shrug.

Roberto groaned feebly as his eyelids flinched. Sofia cried out his name in joy. The *rurale* officer regained consciousness to see the muzzle of Cougar's Colt Dragoon inches from his face. The regulator grimly cocked the hammer of the pistol.

"Play dead or be dead," he warned.

"Si, señor," Roberto nodded.

"We don't want to have to kill a *rurale capitan* in

cold blood, but we can't let our *compañeros* upstairs know we spared you."

"If either of you betray us, we'll kill you *both,*" Shaddrock added. "Roberto here was going to shoot me, so don't press your luck."

"*Gracias,*" Sofia replied, still clutching her husband's head to her naked bosom. "Roberto will pretend to be dead and I will grieve for him until you leave."

"Start grieving," Cougar rasped.

"You realize," Sofia gazed up at Shaddrock with tear-filled eyes. "He was going to kill you because he loves me."

"Sure, lady," the regulator snorted, glancing at the stairs. "I guess he really fell for you all right."

The crowd booed angrily while the man on horseback drove the tip of his lance deep into the shoulder of the snarling black bull in the arena. The beast impotently tried to gouge its horns into the heavy padding that protected the *picador* and his mount. Several spectators pelted the rider with vegetables, half-eaten tacos, and other items. An empty tequila bottle hurled past his sombrero-clad head.

"What are they upset about?" Shaddrock asked his partner.

"He's been sticking the bulls too deep," Cougar replied. "They don't have enough fight left in them to put on a good show when the *matador* arrives."

"Hell," the younger man muttered with disgust. "Those little guys with the capes tire the bull out, then this fella shoves a spear into them and those

147

other characters throw those darts into the animals as well. The bull's half dead by the time the *matador* gets in there with his sword."

"Keep it down," Cougar warned. "These folks get mighty emotional about their bullfights."

"It's one goddamn vicious sport if you ask me," Shaddrock muttered.

"They considered it an art," the senior bounty hunter tilted his head toward the crowd.

"So are shotgun duels," Shaddrock said dryly. "We've sat through four of these butcher's rituals and those *bandidos* haven't shown up yet. What's taking the bastards so long?"

"Don't get impatient," his partner told him. "Larson told Montoya to expect a group of fellers sitting in the second row on the sunny side today. We're here."

"Yeah," the other man sighed watching a *banderillo* deftly dance out of the path of the charging bull. He quickly jammed two *banderilla* darts into the already bleeding beast.

"Do you enjoy the bullfights, *señor?*" a voice asked in English that contained only a trace of a Castilian accent.

"Sure," Shaddrock answered, glancing over his shoulder at the speaker. "I thought the War Between the States was a lot of laughs too."

The face that frowned at the bounty hunter's remark didn't appear to belong to a bandit. Thin and pale, the man wore wire-framed spectacles on the bridge of his straight Creole nose. The hair visible at his temples beneath an inappropriate derby was slate gray and he wore a clean linen suit with a starched collared shirt and a thin tie.

"*Señor* Montoya sent me," he explained.

"You're the contact man?" Cougar asked suspiciously.

"*Si.*" The pale face smiled. "Just call me Francisco. That is not my name, but it will serve, no?"

"If you don't mind, we don't mind," Shaddrock told him.

"I did not expect *señor* Larson to send two *norteamericanos,*" Francisco admitted. "This is why I hesitated to speak to you until now."

"There ain't much to talk about," Cougar commented. "We brought the gun and we want our money. Simple as that."

"Not quite." Francisco sighed. "I am . . . well, I am not an expert concerning firearms. You will have to take the weapon to *señor* Montoya so he can examine it himself. Then you will receive your payment in full."

The *matador* passed his *muleta* cape flamboyantly past the horns of the lunging bull. With four *banderillas* jutting from its massive back, the great beast stumbled and fell to its knees, its tongue hanging limply from its gasping jaws.

"*Repugnante.*" Francisco shook his head. "Disgusting. This bull is a weakling. Have we no *toros bravo* left in Mexico?"

"Maybe you'd be falling down too if you'd been stabbed half a dozen times, fella," Shaddrock snorted.

"You are very soft-hearted for a Comanchero," the Creole said dryly.

"Maybe he's just fond of bull," Cougar replied sharply. "But I ain't—especially if that's what you're giving us, feller."

"*Dispense Vd?*" Francisco asked in a confused tone. "Excuse me?"

The crowd booed as the *matador* thrust the point of his sword into the kneeling bull. The animal bellowed, blood streaming down its back. The *matador* drove the blade through quivering flesh twice more before he punctured the animal's heart. A torrent of crimson gushed from the bull's nostrils and it fell heavily on its side.

"Art, huh?" Shaddrock shook his head. "Think I'll stick with paintings and music."

"What I'm telling you, Francisco"—Cougar continued—"is I don't like the way this setup sounds. We're supposed to go someplace and meet Montoya so he can examine the gun. Why doesn't he come here or send somebody who knows enough about Gatlings to verify that we ain't cheating him?"

"You'll have to ask *señor* Montoya." The go-between shrugged.

"Where does he want this meeting?" Shaddrock inquired, turning to look at Francisco as a team of mules dragged the dead bull from the arena.

"At a *rancho* about four miles from here," the Creole answered, polishing his glasses with a silk handkerchief.

"You go back and tell Montoya we don't accept the terms," Cougar growled. "Tell him . . ."

"I am *señor* Montoya's contact," Francisco declared. "Not *yours*. You do not give me orders."

150

"Maybe I'll give you a busted jaw instead," Cougar said mildly.

"Ole!" the crowd exclaimed as another bull charged into the arena. The go-between mopped his brow with nervous dabs of his handkerchief.

"You will gain nothing by violence, *señor,*" he said.

"Hell." The younger bounty hunter grinned. "It'd be just another art form to these folks."

"Two of Montoya's men will meet you when you leave the bullfights," Francisco told them, his words running together in haste. "I must return to my family now."

"How do they like the rock?" Shaddrock asked.

"I don't understand," the Creole replied. "What rock?"

"The one you crawled out from under, you shit," the bounty hunter answered.

"I resent that remark," Francisco told them, trying to retain some dignity as he rose form his seat.

"You're supposed to." Cougar grinned. "By the way, do you know what a 'shit' is?"

"That is a word in English I am not familiar with," the Creole admitted.

"You got a mirror at home?"

Francisco's features tensed, but he remained silent as he shuffled through the crowd to the exit.

"What do we do now?" Luis asked, seated to the left of Shaddrock.

"I don't like the conditions of this deal," Cougar stated. "Anything could happen at the *rancho.*"

"Ramon says we can trust Montoya," the big Mexican declared. "That's good enough."

151

"Ramon ain't here, feller." The senior bounty hunter shrugged. "So he don't trust him *too* much."

"Shaddrock, you are in command," Luis said. "Do we do the job we came for or are you going to listen to this coward?"

"Your opinion of me might be offensive if you weren't so goddamn stupid, Luis," Cougar remarked in a conversational tone, but his hand rested on the grips of his Colt Dragoon.

"You *gringo bastardo!*" the large man hissed.

"Shut up, both of you!" Shaddrock snapped. "We'll take the Gatling back and explain what happened."

"Maybe I should say *adios* now, Shaddrock." Miguel snickered. "Because Ramon is going to cut your head off for failing in so simple a mission because you have no *huevos.*"

"It doesn't take balls to get yourself killed," Shaddrock told the Comancheros. "If we blunder into a trap, we could lose the Gatling guns as well as our lives. Where's the profit in that?"

"You question Ramon's judgment?" Luis inquired with a cold smile.

"Well," Shaddrock sighed. "If we run into trouble, just remember I tried to keep us out of it."

The crowd roared with disapproval as the *picador* once again dug the point of his lance deep into the shoulder of a bull. Snorting in pain and anger, the wounded beast hopelessly gouged its horns into the quilted armor of the *picador's* horse. The man shoved harder and the entire blade and part of the *pica's* shaft sunk inside the bull's flesh. With a great bleat of agony, the animal staggered and collapsed in a

152

twitching heap.

"Carnicero!" a voice shouted. "Butcher!"

The report of a pistol echoed from the bleachers. Blood splattered the *picador's* colorful costume as a bullet drilled into his chest. The man cried out and toppled awkwardly from the back of his mount. Spectators turned to the uniformed figure who stood triumphantly waving his smoking pistol overhead. he wore the insignia of a *Federale* colonel. The crowd applauded vigorously and the killer bowed in response.

"That's what I call a real art critic," Cougar muttered.

THIRTEEN

The long ribbon of worn earth could only be called a road by those who'd made it—*peones* with burros and tiny two-wheeled carts. The two *bandidos* who led the way, rode the rough uphill path with the ease of experience and the benefit of stocky mustangs better suited for the task than most breeds of horses. Mounted on less sure-footed steeds, the Comancheros had trouble keeping up with their guides and the wagon endured even more trouble as the mules protested every step of the way. It was obvious Montoya had chosen a remote location for his headquarters, a fact that offered little comfort to Shaddrock and Cougar.

As the great orange sun began its descent in the distance, they finally approached the *rancho*. The *villa* measured more than a city block in diameter. The great house was a colossus of adobe and slate with tinted glass and red oak doors imported from California. Orchards of various small trees formed a semicircle around the *villa*, and the stables contained horses bred more for pleasure than transportation.

The Garcia family had constructed the *villa* in a classical "Old World" style. Although considered Spanish, the architecture revealed the Islamic influence of the Moors with the teardrop-shaped roofs of the ornamental towers that extended above the main building. Perhaps Umberto Garcia should have added a moat and drawbridge as well. His home had proved to be an easy conquest for Thomas Montoya and his *bandidos.*

The sound of drunken laughter and slurred singing extended from the *villa* to the travelers. Even in the feeble light of dusk, Shaddrock and Cougar saw the bullet scars on the whitewashed adobe. Two dark brown stains of dried blood marked one wall like a macabre address number.

The unexpected report of a rifle knifed through the sounds of the celebration within the house. The bounty hunters' hands flew to the butts of their revolvers in response, but the orange flame from one of the towers streaked harmlessly into the sky and revealed the *sombrero* clad sentry stationed there.

"Relax, *amigos,*" one of the bandit guides urged with a chuckle. "It is only a signal. One shot to let them know Carlos and I have returned from Monterey. The guard would fire two shots if the *Federales* decided to pay us a visit. Is simple, no?"

"One hell of a doorbell," Shaddrock muttered, easing his fingers from the Police Colt under his left arm.

The great twin doors of the *villa* swung open abruptly, oak slapping adobe. Half a dozen men dressed in ill-treated clothing and sombreros stomped from the entrance. A pear-shaped figure led the procession—of average height with a narrow chest and a fleshy middle, his appearance would have been quite unimpressive without bandoliers and pistols on

155

his hips. A cigar that seemed too large for his mouth, jutted from his dense black beard.

"Ah! I see you have delivered our visitors safe and sound, eh?" he declared in a loud abrasive voice. "Which one of you is in charge?"

"The *Anglo* with the blue eyes," a bandit replied. "He does not understand our language so you will have to speak through the *gringo* next to him."

"Oh?" Thomas Montoya frowned, shifting the oversized cigar in the mouth hidden somewhere under his beard. "You are not a *mejicano?*" His voice revealed disappointment as he looked at Cougar.

"Nobody's perfect," the senior bounty hunter replied in Spanish.

"Do not tell that to your *jefe.*" The bandit leader laughed. "Ramon thinks he is! I've known him for a long time. Ramon is as loco as a scorpion that goes berserk in the sun and stings itself to death, but he is clever, that one."

Several *bandidos* moved to the wagon and hauled the coffins off the vehicle. Others surrounded the Comancheros, their expressions revealing distrust, annoyance, amusement, and indifference. Yet, not a single weapon was aimed at the gunrunners. Shaddrock and Cougar slowly climbed from the rig, the latter holding his shotgun loosely in one hand.

"Bring the boxes inside," Montoya instructed. "Let's unwrap this gift at the banquet table like a Christmas present, no?"

"Just remember it isn't a gift," Cougar said quietly. "We're here to make a sale. You're getting a unique and dependable firearm and it has a price tag on it."

156

"Si," the bandit chief sighed. "You are a practical man, *senor."* Montoya's face brightened and a glimpse of yellow teeth appeared between the beard and the cigar stump. "But you are still my guests. We will celebrate my new Gatling gun in my new house. Come."

The bounty hunters and their Comanchero companions followed the *bandidos* into the *villa.* Bullet holes peppered the walls of a spacious hall. Paintings had been ripped into unrecognizable shreds and the jagged debris of shattered vases littered the floor. The stale odor of urine hovered from a small potted palm tree someone had relieved himself on.

Montoya guided his visitors into a large sitting room. Evidence of barbaric behavior was everywhere. Fine quality furniture had been slashed with knives, hacked with machetes, and ravaged by bullets. Expensive chairs were broken into kindling for the fireplace. Blood and scattered feathers revealed where the *bandidos* had slaughtered chickens and roasted them over the flames.

"Did you know Ramon came from a house such as this?" Montoya inquired, turning slowly with his arms wide to indicate their surroundings. "It was not owned by his family, of course. His mother was a servant in a *villa* not unlike this one. I guess that is where he got his taste for expensive things.

"Now, me." The *bandido* theatrically jammed all ten fingers into his narrow chest. "I was born in a *peone* village. All we had was poverty and hunger. That is why I hate these rich *bastardos* and I glory in the destruction of the trinkets they hold so dear. It is poetic justice, no?"

"What's he saying?" Shaddrock asked his partner, unable to understand Montoya's speech.

"He's being a profound asshole," Cougar replied dryly.

"The wealthy have things like this"—Montoya contemptuously kicked the remnants of a sofa—"while the poor sleep on straw mats with bedbugs and lice for company. They let their extra food rot while *peone* children starve. They build big houses with more rooms than they know what to do with and the *peones* are crammed into huts like cattle in a butcher yard."

"Don't tell this guy about your family back in Philadelphia," Cougar warned Shaddrock, briefly translating the *bandido's* remarks.

"This fat hypocrite doesn't look like he's missed any meals lately," the younger regulator snorted. "What the hell has he been doing for these *peones* he cries about?"

"He talks about them." Cougar shrugged.

Four bandits placed the coffins on the floor and pried the lids open. Montoya smiled at the sight of the disassembled Gatling gun. He knelt beside the cluster of iron barrels, stroking them tenderly as one might a woman's thigh.

"And you know what the *Federales* do for *peones?*" he asked fiercely. "They do nothing! But for the rich ... ah, for the rich they provide protection and they bow with respect in honor of the swine who play while others starve."

"What's he yapping about now?" Shaddrock inquired.

158

"I can't repeat it," Cougar said dryly. "It's too sad."

"But with this gun"—the bandit chief smiled, sliding his fingers along the Gatling's frame—"I will be able to teach the *Federales* a lesson. They will respect Tomas Emmanual Montoya."

"There is no ammunition for the gun, *jefe!*" a tall, fence-post lean *bandido* exclaimed.

"Estupido!" Montoya snapped. "I have all the bullets I will need and Ceasare knows how to assemble the Gatling. He will teach me to use it so I can personally blast those uniformed bootlickers to hell!"

"Reckon everybody needs a goal in life," Cougar muttered in English.

"But now," the bandit leader declared, rising from the mistreated carpet. "Now we will join the others in the dining hall to celebrate this night of nights. We have tequila, food, and women waiting for us there."

"Keep away from the women," Cougar told his partner.

"I'd rather keep away from the tequila and food." Shaddrock frowned.

The dining room had once been equipped with a splendid chandelier, an antique china closet, and a buffet. All had been smashed and discarded by the new residents. The long walnut table remained intact, although its linen cloth had been removed and the surface was marred by knife cuts. The more literate bandits had carved their initials and Spanish obscenities in the wood.

Fourteen men surrounded the table. Some sat in the

159

thronelike chairs provided by the Garcia family, but most were content to sit on crates and barrels. The *bandidos* glanced up from their plates of tortillas, tostadas, and beans long enough to smile or nod. Then they attacked their food with fork and knife as though making certain each portion was dead before it entered their mouths.

"Hector! Ricardo!" the bandit chief snapped. "Get out of those chairs and let our guests have an honorable position at the table!"

Two disgruntled *bandidos* rose in response, uttering surly remarks under their breath. Shaddrock occupied a vacant chair at one end of the table while Cougar sat between two unwashed outlaws. The senior bounty hunter laid the shotgun across his lap and nodded at a grinning, bearded face across from him.

Montoya waddled to the head of the table and sank into a chair, leaning back wearily. "That pig Garcia kept many servants," he told his visitors. "He treated them badly and they are very grateful to me for liberating them."

"A *bandido* Abe Lincoln," Shaddrock remarked after Cougar translated the outlaw's remarks.

The younger regulator glanced at the *bandidos* seated to his left and right at the corners of the table. One leered at him mockingly while the other avoided looking at the American as he shoveled tostadas and beans into his mouth. Luis and the other Comancheros were supplied with boxes to join the others at the table.

"Now, the serfs of Umberto Garcia serve me and my men willingly," Montoya claimed, tossing the soggy corpse of his cigar over his shoulder to gather up a bottle of tequila.

"Nice to see somebody has a sense of gratitude these days," Cougar replied, barely keeping the sarcasm from his voice.

Seven men, dressed in clean white shirts and chinos, entered the dining hall. Three wore thick drooping mustaches, but all had recently shaved their jaws and cheeks. Each servant carried a dark bottle on a dinner plate in one hand.

"I told them we were expecting guests," Montoya declared. "Take the tequila and fill those plates and join us in our festival."

"Now what's he saying?" Shaddrock asked with disgust.

"Never mind," Cougar said in a casual tone. "I think we're in trouble."

"How's that?" the younger man inquired as a *peon* placed a plate and bottle before him. The other servants did the same for Cougar and the Comancheros.

"There's seven of us," Cougar stated. "And *seven* servants."

"Oh, shit," Shaddrock whispered.

At that moment, the *bandidos* disguised as servants, produced their knives and garrotes. Montoya's plan to kill his guests at the dinner table was a partial success. Manuel Santos, a young Comanchero, died with a bottle of tequila in his mouth. As he raised the liquor to his lips, the servant standing beside him drove the blade of his dirk between Santos' ribs. The Comanchero's teeth clamped down on the glass hard, literally biting through the neck of the bottle.

161

Miguel didn't have time to say grace either. A phony *peon* tossed the thick cord of a garrote over the Yaqui half-breed's head and crossed his wrists. The strangler braced a knee against the back of Miguel's chair and pulled hard. The rope constricted swiftly around the Comanchero's neck, biting into carotid arteries and windpipe. Miguel's arms slashed desperately at his opponent, but the *bandido* leaned back out of reach. Soon his struggles ceased as he died where he sat.

The servant next to Shaddrock thrust his knife at the American's chest, planning to penetrate his heart with a single stroke. But the blade stabbed air as the bounty hunter powered himself backward, purposely tipping over his chair. Man and furniture crashed to the floor, but the regulator ignored the sudden jolt of the fall and yanked both Police Colts from their holsters.

Before the false *peon* could recover from his surprise the pistol in Shaddrock's right hand roared. A .36 caliber lead ball ripped into the *bandido's* solar plexus, burning a path upward to the heart. The impact hurtled the man backward to collapse unceremoniously on the table, blood splashing his white cotton shirt.

Cougar's Bowie knife was already out of its sheath when he glanced at the servant behind him. The man held a garrote in his fists, prepared to strangle his intended victim. The bounty hunter leaned to the left as the strangling cord descended. Rope slapped the backrest of Cougar's chair an instant before the regulator's arm rose. The *bandido* saw the wicked blade of

Cougar's Bowie rocketing toward his face. It was the last sight he beheld before he died. The steel point bit into the strangler's left eye, slicing the delicate orb to puncture the brain. A terrible scream escaped from the man's lips as he staggered back, dropped his garrote and clawed hopelessly at the knife that jutted from his bloodied eyesocket. He died with both hands still clutching the staghorn handle of the Bowie.

Shoving his chair aside, Cougar dropped to one knee, the sawed-off Greener filling his hands. The grinning *bandido* seated across from the bounty hunter had begun to rise, dragging a Navy Colt from its holster. A shotgun barrel exploded a vicious load of buckshot under the table. A shriek of agony competed with the echo of the blast as pellets tore into the bandit's legs, turning his shins, turning the lower legs into useless stumps of pulverized muscle and splintered bone.

Luis caught the arm behind a thrusting knife blade as another servant tried to dispatch the huge Mexican. Bellowing with rage, the Comanchero swung the would-be killer over the width of the table, throwing the man as though he were a bag of grain. The *bandido* crashed into two of his comrades as they began to rise and paw at holstered sidearms. All three men toppled to the floor.

Still lying on his back, Shaddrock's arms formed a wide V as the two *bandidos* seated at the corner of the table jumped upright and drew their weapons. The bounty hunter's Police Colts snarled with one great voice. A .36 projectile bore through the center of one bandit's throat, bursting his Adam's apple and windpipe before it exploded in a jagged exit hole at the base of his neck. The man's hand flew to the crimson stream that spewed from the horrid wound. His eyes bulged as the cold reality of death closed in around him. He sank to his knees, spitting blood in an attempt to pray before life fled his unwashed body.

Shaddrock's other pistol shot also found its target. A bullet struck the second *bandido* under the nose. The man's upper jaw burst into a pulped mess of blood, bone, and rotted teeth. The force of the round sent him backward to fall into the lap of a startled *companero.*

The bandits at both sides of the kneeling Cougar slid back their chairs to attack the bounty hunter. Pivoting on his right knee, Cougar drove the butt of his Greener into the closest man's lower abdomen, hammering hard walnut an inch above his opponent's groin. With a gasp, the Mexican convulsed in his chair. His intestines seemed to be on fire and vomit rose to his throat like a tequila flavored volcano.

The second barrel of the shotgun boomed as the other bandit jerked a Walker Colt from a belly holster. Buckshot smashed into the outlaw at close range. The holster was reduced to mangled, shredded leather—his belly suffered a similar fate. Propelled by the force of the blast, an invisible cable seemed to jerk the *bandido* from his chair and hurled his body to the floor. Cougar then slammed the iron barrels of his Greener into the side of the puking man's head, cracking his skull at the temple.

"Crowly!" Luis shouted.

The bounty hunter saw the big Comanchero gripping the edge of the table in his huge hands. He quickly joined the Mexican hulk. For once, the two men agreed on a choice of action. They pushed hard and turned over the long table even as the remaining *bandidos* scattered from their chairs and opened fire.

Bullets punched through the wooden table top like lead hornets. One creased Luis' left triceps, nicking the surface of his skin. Another projectile tugged at Cougar's sombrero. While *bandido* rounds continued to puncture their inadequate shelter, Shaddrock scrambled over to them on all fours, his Police Colts in his fists.

"So much for Ramon Larson as a judge of character," he rasped, hugging the floor as a volley of bullets splintered wood.

"Yeah," Cougar agreed. "Montoya wants to have his Gatling gun cake and the seven thousand pesos too."

Pedro Gonzales, one of the Comancheros, crawled to them, blood seeping from a minor wound in his right calf. "They got Orlando," he announced. "The *bastardos* cut him down as he . . ."

The rest of his sentence was lost amid another concentrated salvo of gunfire by the *bandidos*. Bullets snarled through the shield at a lower angle, some smashing into floorboards near the huddled men. Shaddrock returned fire with a Police Colt and quickly ducked down.

"Those scum-suckers reacted pretty slow at the table," he growled. "Probably because they relied on that fake servant trick to take care of us."

"I think they've been drinking too much too," Cougar added. "But they ain't so drunk they don't realize this table won't stop any bullets. They can just shoot it to pieces—along with us."

"Then what do we do?" Luis asked fearfully.

"I guess we're gonna die," Cougar replied simply.

Another eruption of gunshots echoed within the dining hall, the sound threatening to shake the walls apart by its volume alone. The bounty hunters and the Comancheros ground their teeth, expecting to feel the agony of burning lead ripping into their flesh. Yet, not a single bullet struck the table. Several screams pierced the roar of the firearms. Then everything ceased—gunfire, heart beats, time itself drifted into a realm of unnatural quiet.

"What the hell?" Shaddrock wondered aloud, breaking the spell of silence.

Suspecting a trick, the four men remained behind the table, weapons ready and their pulses racing at a crazy tempo. Then several figures stomped around the overturned furniture. The defenders nearly opened fire on the intruders until they saw the tan uniforms and caps of the *Federales.* However, the grim expressions of the soldiers told them the patrol wasn't there to rescue them. The *Federales* pointed their guns at the group.

"Hold on!" Shaddrock urged. "Er . . . *esperar uno momento.* We aren't *bandidos.*" He turned to Cougar. "Talk to these guys."

"We know who you are," a sleek, ferret-faced lieutenant declared in excellent English. He folded his arms akimbo on his chest as he strolled closer. "And *what* you are. A mutual friend of ours—you know him as Francisco—told us all about you Comanchero swine."

"That little shit," Cougar groaned.

"Of course, we hadn't anticipated that you'd be considerate enough to create such a fine distraction for us when we raided the *villa*."

"Hope you liked it," Shaddrock said with a weak grin.

"You mad dogs couldn't help fighting among yourselves no?" the *Federale teniente* stated with a smug smile. "I don't suppose I have to inform you that you are all under arrest."

"Aw, hell." Cougar shook his head with dismay.

FOURTEEN

Cavillo Prison was located approximately seven miles north of Monterrey. A twenty-foot-high stone wall surrounded the solid adobe brick buildings within. Cavillo was a *Federale* prison guarded by a company of men. Sentries stalked the walls and a Gatling gun had been mounted at the front gate, its barrels aimed at the exercise yard below. Shaddrock glanced up at the weapon and the uniformed guard behind it. *I wish I'd never seen one of those damn things,* he thought sourly.

The Gatling he had helped smuggle across the border, still lay disassembled in the coffins. A bleary eyed, unshaven officer nearly lost his balance as he leaned over the boxes to examine the contents. Although he wore uniform trousers and boots, his upper torso was clad only in a ragged long john shirt. Shaddrock, Cougar, the two Comancheros, and the three *bandidos* who'd survived the gun battle at the *rancho* would not have known the man's rank if the soldiers surrounding them had not addressed him by it.

"*Capitan* Sanches?" the young lieutenant who'd captured the group began. "Do you know what that is?"

"*Seguro!*" the other officer replied sharply, al-

168

though he weaved drunkenly as he straightened his back. "It is . . ." he glanced down at the open coffins once more and then pointed at the Gatling on the wall. "One of those things, no?"

"Si, Capitan," the lieutenant said patiently. "These Comancheros brought the gun to Montoya to sell it to the pig. They are no better than the *bandidos.*"

"Maybe worse." Sanchez nodded. "You have done well to bring them here, *Teniente* Platas. I shall see to it these misbegotten wolf pups of diseased *putas* remain behind bars until it is time for their trial and execution. Relay this information to General Martinez when you make your report, *por favor.*"

"Of course, *Capitan,*" Platas agreed. "And thank you for taking these *bastardos* off my hands."

Sanchez belched in reply.

Lieutenant Platas saluted crisply. The captain didn't pay attention, so the younger officer merely told his men to mount up. Platas and his patrol rode from the prison, hauling the confiscated Gatling on the back of the wagon the Comancheros had supplied.

"You men listen to me," Sanchez ordered in a slurred voice. "This is Cavillo Prison and I am its commandant. No one can escape from here, so do not even consider such things. I am a hard man and I rule with a hand of iron." He clenched a fist and stared at it as though he'd never seen his knuckles before. "You try to escape and you'll be shot. You disobey an order and I'll have you shot. Sometimes we shoot prisoners just for entertainment, so you better hope we don't get bored, eh?"

He laughed stupidly at his own joke. Half a dozen

guards, who trained their rifles on the captives, joined in their commander's laughter until he broke into a spittle-spraying cough. Sanchez shook his head and cursed under his breath.

"Capitan?" a muscular young sergeant spoke. "Do you want us to take the prisoners to their cell?"

"Si, si," Sanchez answered wearily. "They know the rules now. Get them out of my sight. I do not feel well and I think I'd better lie down for a while."

The captain staggered to his office as the NCO turned to his troops. "You heard the *capitan.* Let's put these animals in a cage like they deserve. *Vamanos!"*

All seven prisoners, Comanchero and *bandido* alike were shoved into the same cell. Although large enough to allow the men to move without trampling each other's feet, it hadn't been swept out since it was last occupied and the stench of old urine filled their nostrils. There was no window for ventilation—just three solid adobe walls, a door of iron bars, and a stone floor. A private with a baton in his fist marched wearily back and forth in the corridor on the other side of the bars.

"If only those *idiotas* dressed as *peones* had killed you Comancheros we would have heard the rifle shots of the sentries back at the *villa* and none of this would have happened," Tomas Montoya complained bitterly.

"If you think we were such lousy guests," Cougar replied dryly, "don't invite us to your next party."

"I'll kill you, you son of a whore!" Luis snarled, charging across the cell at Montoya.

170

The big Comanchero's hands closed around Montoya's throat. Luis shoved his victim back into a corner and lifted the fat bandit off the floor. Montoya's feet kicked helplessly in the air and his eyes bulged in terror as the giant Mexican began to literally hang him using bare hands for a noose.

"No, Luis!" Shaddrock ordered.

The Comanchero hulk ignored him. The bounty hunters, Pedro Gonzales, and the two lesser bandits had to join together to pull Luis away from his intended victim. Montoya slumped to the floor in a gasping heap.

"Damn it," Shaddrock snapped. "We've got enough stink in here without having his corpse smelling up the place."

"Bastardo!" Luis hissed, spewing a glob of saliva into Montoya's still-purple face.

"Call him names and spit on him," Cougar allowed. "But don't kill him yet. If we're gonna get out of here, we *might* need him."

"Do you have a plan for us to escape from this taco prison?" Shaddrock asked, moving to his partner's side.

"Not really." The senior bounty hunter shrugged. "But letting Luis strangle Montoya won't help us."

"Great." The younger man clucked his tongue. "I wasn't in favor of this job from the beginning. Remember? I called it a suicide . . ."

"Watch your mouth," Cougar advised, reminding his partner that Luis and Pedro understood English. "If only we had a weapon."

"We do," Shaddrock replied. "Though I don't know

171

what good it'll do." He unbuttoned his fly. "I managed to shove it into my pants when the *Federales* showed up. Guess where I got that idea?"

"But this time the jail break is for real," Cougar whispered. "Come on, get it out of there."

"What the hell do you think I'm doing?" the younger man snapped.

"Are you *gringos* doing what it appears you are?" Luis asked in a dazed voice. He stared at Shaddrock as he reached inside his crotch.

"Behave yourself, Luis," Cougar told him. "You ain't been in prison long enough to get such notions."

The huge Mexican bared his teeth, offended by the insult to his *machismo*. "Someday I kill you, Crowly!"

"Uh-huh." The senior bounty hunter nodded, unimpressed by the threat.

"Here it is," Shaddrock announced, pulling his brass knuckle-dusters from his trousers.

"Aw, shit," Cougar muttered. "I figured you had your derringer in there."

"I didn't bring it." His partner shrugged.

"Why didn't you, dumb ass?"

"Why didn't you bring your boot pistol, fuckhead?"

"Never mind," Cougar rasped.

"Well, I don't suppose this thing will do much good," Shaddrock admitted. "Unless we can punch our way out of this place."

"Maybe we can," the senior man mused, watching the sentry stroll past the cell.

"No more jokes about the science of pugilism,'

172

Shaddrock urged.

"Keep an eye on that feller," his partner said, pointing at the corridor. "When he heads back this way, let me know with a nod."

The younger bounty hunter didn't ask why, he merely stationed himself by the door. Cougar stepped to the middle of the cell, watching Shaddrock while the others observed the pair with absolute bewilderment.

Then Shaddrock nodded.

"Montoya," Cougar whispered harshly, gesturing for the bandit chief to come closer.

"What do you want, *gringo?*" Montoya demanded as he approached the regulator.

"I told you to keep your mouth shut about the gold!" Cougar shouted in Spanish.

His fist crashed into the startled bandido's beard, knuckles connecting with jawbone hard. The punch propelled Montoya into a wall. Once again, he slumped to the floor in an undignified seated position, legs splayed, his eyes open and glassy. The sentry stopped by the barred door and stared inside.

The other two bandits helped their dazed chief to his feet. Shaddrock stuffed his hands into his pants pockets, clenching the brass knuckles in one fist. Cougar glanced at the guard and shrugged.

"Just an argument," he explained. "Forget it."

The sentry moved from the bars and hurried down the corridor. Shaddrock walked up to his partner. "And what the hell was the purpose of that?" he inquired.

"Oh, I tried to put a bee in our keeper's ear," Cougar

answered. He translated what he'd shouted before he hit Montoya.

"What's that going to accomplish?" the other bounty hunter asked.

"That *Federale* flunky just ran off to report this incident to somebody. Who do you think he'll tell it to?"

"Probably the NCO in charge of the watch."

"Right." Cougar nodded. "And what will he do?"

"If everything goes through the chain of command, he'll report it to the officer in charge who'll pass it on to Captain Sanchez."

"That's what he's *supposed* to do," the other man agreed. "But since Sanchez is a drunken incompetent, the morale of the troops in this place is probably lousy and most *Federales* of every rank are about half-*bandido* anyway. I'm hoping the sergeant will be tempted by the suggestion of available gold."

"Yeah." Shaddrock smiled. "And why tell the captain and maybe lose the loot when he only has to share it with one or two of his men."

"But first they have to find out where the gold is," the senior regulator added. "That means they'll be back to talk to us about it."

Five minutes later, the sentry, another private, and the young sergeant who'd marched the prisoners to their cell appeared at the door. All three men were armed. The noncom aimed a pistol between the bars and ordered the captives to move back.

"Which one was it, Rodriguez?" he asked the sentry, inserting a key in the cell door.

"That one mentioned *los oro*," Rodriguez replied, pointing the bayonet at the end of his carbine to indicate Cougar. "And he hit the fat one for speaking of it, *Sargento* Vargas."

"Then we will talk to the *hombre* whose lips already seem eager to tell us about it," Vargas replied with a thin smile. "Come with us, fat one."

Montoya hesitated. The sergeant cocked the hammer of his revolver. Reluctantly, the bandit leader shuffled from the cell. Vargas locked the cage door and the trio of soldiers escorted Montoya down the corridor. Their voices reached the men left in the cell.

"Now, tell us about *los oro, amigo,*" Vargas said pleasantly.

"There isn't any gold. . ." Montoya began. The sound of a fist striking flesh interrupted him.

"Don't be stubborn," Vargas warned.

"But there isn't any. . ." another blow terminated the bandit's words.

Shaddrock turned to Cougar as he listened to the soldiers crudely interrogate their prisoner, employing fists and gun butts more than words. "That Montoya is too tough for them," he remarked dryly. "They'll never beat any information out of him."

"Nope," Cougar agreed. "Reckon they'll want to have a chat with me pretty soon."

"Sure hope your plan works."

"We'll find out."

Half an hour later, the soldiers dragged the bruised and bleeding unconscious form of Tomas Montoya back to the cell. The sergeant unlocked the door and the enlisted men threw the *bandido* chief inside like a pile of dirty laundry. Both his eyes were swollen and bruised. His nose had been broken and his black beard

175

was stained with scarlet.

"This man would not talk and you can see what it gained him," Sergeant Vargas declared. "Perhaps the rest of you will be more willing to converse with us now."

The captives didn't reply.

"All right, you!" The NCO thrust the barrel of his Colt at Cougar. "Come with us."

"No!" the bounty hunter exclaimed, cowering back into a corner, his eyes wide with mock terror. "I won't! You'll have to shoot me first!"

"If we shoot you *first,* you won't be able to tell us anything, *estupido,"* Vargas snorted. "Rodriguez! Moreno! Drag that coward's *nalga* out here."

The two soldiers slung the carbines to their shoulders and entered the cell. They stomped closer to the bounty hunter, their faces stiff with annoyance and determination. Suddenly, Cougar thrust his arms high in surrender.

"All right!" he cried. "I'll talk!"

"Where is the gold?" Vargas snapped, stepping across the threshold. His attention was centered on Cougar and he failed to notice Shaddrock as the regulator gradually moved closer.

"It's right here," Cougar replied, dropping his hands and looking at the floor. "Right there at our feet."

Confused and baffled, the soldiers' eyes fell to the floor. Cougar seized the opportunity created by the distraction. He stepped forward and swung a powerful upper cut to Private Moreno's jaw. The fist forced the trooper's head to snap back and would have

176

knocked him five feet if the bounty hunter hadn't grabbed the man's tunic. Cougar's knee whipped between the stunned man's legs. Moreno wilted to the stone floor with a rasping moan.

Sergeant Vargas cursed under his breath and tried to thumb back the hammer of his Colt. Shaddrock moved in quickly and chopped his brass reinforced fist down on the noncom's wrist. Bone snapped and the revolver fell from his grasp. Vargas barely had time to feel the pain of his broken wrist before Shaddrock jabbed a short, hard punch to the point of his jaw. The knuckle-dusters cracked against flesh and bone. The sergeant hurtled from the cell and fell to the corridor floor—unconscious.

Private Rodriguez desperately attempted to unsling his weapon, but Luis didn't let him. The big Mexican slammed a mallet-sized fist into the soldier's midsection. Rodriguez doubled up and Luis seized him by the nape of the neck and the seat of the trousers. With a mighty heave, the giant Comanchero drove the trooper into the nearest wall head first. The skull split on impact with a grotesque, wet *thump.* Private Rodriguez slid to the floor, smearing brains and blood on the adobe.

"Looks like I get to play sergeant again," Shaddrock commented, shoving the NCO's pistol into his belt. He dragged Vargas into the cell and knelt to unbutton his uniform jacket.

"This guy's clothes will fit me," Cougar announced, gathering up Moreno's Spencer. "Pedro, I think you're a better choice to wear Rodriguez's uniform than Luis."

"What about us?" one of the *bandidos* demanded.

"Don't worry about it." Cougar smiled, stepping closer. "We ain't forgetting about you."

He suddenly smashed the walnut stock of the carbine into the side of the bandit's head. The man dropped with a groan and lay still. The remaining member of Montoya's gang panicked and ran for the cell door. Luis seized the man from behind. The Comanchero picked up the *bandido* and held him horizontal at chest level. Terrified, the man screamed as Luis dropped to one knee. He brought the small of the bandit's back down across his other knee. The cry of desperation became a shriek of agony. Then the man with the broken spine twitched twice and died.

"Jesus," Shaddrock muttered, slipping on the *Federale* sergeant's tunic. "That Luis is one mean son of a bitch."

"I don't know," Cougar replied dryly. "He doesn't mind giving a feller a break once in a while."

FIFTEEN

"*Capitan* Sanchez has ordered us to inspect the arms room," Cougar told the corporal stationed by the munitions building.

The soldier frowned, staring at the tall, pale-skinned sergeant and the man who spoke *espanol* with a strange accent and seemed too old to still be a private. He didn't recognize either man and there were less than a hundred assigned to Cavillo Prison.

"Do you have any identification?" he asked the blue-eyed NCO, wondering why the man had remained silent while a mere private did the talking.

"*Si,*" Shaddrock replied, reaching into a pocket.

His brass-knuckled fist swung into the unprepared corporal's bread basket. The Mexican folded with a grunt. Cougar's right arm rose. His semiclosed fist chopped into the trooper's mastoid behind the ear and the man collapsed with a sigh.

"Is that one of those Indian fighting tricks you learned from those Johnny Reb Cherokees during the war?" Shaddrock inquired.

"Yeah," Cougar replied, taking the keys from the senseless soldier.

"What's it called?"

"A rabbit punch is a rabbit punch whatever you call

179

it," the senior bounty hunter answered.

Unlocking the arms room, they dragged the corporal inside and gestured to Luis and Pedro, who waited in the shadows of the cell block section. The Comancheros rushed to the building, taking care to avoid detection by the sentries on the wall. Luckily, clouds covered most of the moon and stars, contributing to the darkness.

"Hot damn!" Shaddrock exclaimed when he located his Police Colts and shoulder holster rig among the weapons piled within.

"Luis, that corporal isn't as big as you, but his clothes will have to do," Cougar stated. "Take his tunic and put it on—and *don't* kill him!"

"Are you squeamish, Crowly?" the big Mexican snorted.

"I don't see any sense in killing somebody if you don't have to," the senior regulator replied, reclaiming his gunbelt from the pile.

"You seem to forget *señor* Shaddrock is in charge . . ."

"Put on the guy's jacket," Shaddrock instructed "And then leave the poor bastard alone."

"Look at all these guns!" Pedro smiled, staring at the Army carbines in their racks. "We could make a lot of money selling them to *Indios* and small outlaw gangs."

"Just take a long gun and a sidearm and some ammunition for each," Cougar told him. "We'll be lucky to get out of here alive, let alone loaded down with excess merchandise."

"And don't use your guns unless you have to,"

Shaddrock added. "We're no match for a company of soldiers, so we don't want any shooting if we can avoid it."

"What do we do now?" Luis asked. He held a Spencer in his fist. The corporal's jacket sleeves barely fit over his bulging upper arms and the buttons were unfastened to accommodate his barrel chest.

"We borrow four horses from the stables," Cougar replied, checking the loads of his Greener shotgun. "Then we hope it's too dark for anyone to get a good look at us and we try to bullshit our way through the front gate."

"I have a question Coug . . . Crowly," Shaddrock said. "How do we bullshit our way out of here?"

"I can only think of one explanation for us leaving the post at this hour of the night that the guards might believe," Cougar answered.

Ramon Larson tilted back his head and laughed. "You told them *Capitan* Sanchez was sending you out to get him more tequila?"

"We also claimed we were going to pack up four kegs of beer in ice for the troops," Cougar added. "You should have seen those gates fly open then."

Shaddrock, Cougar, Luis, and Pedro had returned to the Comanchero camp the following morning. They spoke with Ramon Larson in the center of the bivouac area, explaining their experiences to the outlaw leader.

"Incredible," the Comanchero boss remarked. "If you didn't have the *federale* uniforms to prove it, I'd be tempted to think the whole story was a fabrication."

Marie stepped from the tent behind Larson. Her eyes met Shaddrock's. He grinned and she smiled in return, an expression of longing filling her lovely features.

"But it happened just as you have been told, Ramon," Pedro insisted. "We are fortunate to have escaped with our lives to return here. It was the cunning of *señors* Shaddrock and Crowly that saved us. Without them, we would probably have wound up like Miguel, Orlando, and Santos. God rest their souls."

"God, eh?" the atheist Larson chuckled. "Well, God did not smile on you all that much. The only amusing part of this story is the end."

His expression darkened as he turned to Shaddrock and Cougar. "You didn't get any money for the Gatling *and* you lost the gun as well!"

"Wait a minute, Ramon!" Shaddrock snapped in response. "Crowly and I didn't like the way Montoya had the deal set up. We were in favor of pulling out and returning the Gatling to you, but the others insisted we make the exchange. They said *you* vouched for Montoya. He was your buddy, Ramon. You figured we could trust him, so if somebody fucked up on this deal—it was *you!*"

Larson's eyes expanded in their sockets. He seemed too stunned by Shaddrock's remark to have any emotional room for anger. The other Comancheros glanced from their leader to the bounty hunter, holding their collective breath as they waited for Larson's reaction to such harsh criticism. Marie covered her mouth to repress a gasp, her eyes filled with shock and dread. Quint's lipless mouth formed a sneer. Cougar shook his head as he realized his partner would never stop taking damn fool chances.

"*Huevos,*" the Comanchero chief stated flatly. "You do indeed have *huevos,* Shaddrock."

He paced slowly, like a shark circling its prey, but his expression revealed amusement. "That is what I like about you, Shaddrock. You tell me what you think and you don't care if I like it or not. *Huevos!* Balls!" Larson strolled to the tent and smiled at Marie. "That's what you like about him too, no?"

"Ramon . . ." she began, but the back of his hand struck her face so hard it spun the girl around. Larson grabbed her long red hair and twisted it cruelly. Shaddrock stepped forward, but Cougar put a hand on his shoulder to restrain him.

"Getting yourself killed won't help her," the senior bounty hunter whispered.

"You thought you could fuck with another man and I would not learn of it?" the Comanchero leader hissed into Marie's ear. "Wrong, little *puta!* I know what you and Shaddrock have done. You have always been a whore and you always shall remain one!"

He shoved the girl away from his tent. "You aren't my woman any longer, slut!" Larson declared. "You move in with the other *putas.* If you want to spread your legs to other men, you can service my Comancheros whenever they feel the need for a cheap fuck from a cheap whore!"

Several men cheered as they rubbed their crotches with expectation. Wesley Quint's hand rested on the ivory grips of his Smith & Wesson. He turned to Larson. "What do you want done with Shaddrock?" the gunfighter asked eagerly.

"What do you mean, Quint?" the Comanchero chief answered, blinking as though baffled by the question.

"He was messing around with your woman . . ."

"She offered herself to him like a bitch in heat." Larson shrugged. "How can he be blamed for following his desires for an attractive woman?"

"Hell, Ramon!" Quint growled. "The other men in this camp didn't screw around with her . . ."

"That's because they didn't have the *huevos* to do so," the Comanchero replied.

"I'm not afraid of you, damn it!" the pistolman declared. "But I never would have hopped in the sack with Marie because she belonged to you."

"And she never would have offered it to you because you're too ugly," the outlaw chief said curtly. "Besides, you're the only man in this camp who tries to abstain from everything—tobacco, tequila, women, life itself. Don't expect others to take a vow of celibacy because you have decided to, Quint."

The others listened to the conversation with astonishment. None were more surprised than Shaddrock and Cougar.

"I never heard such crap in my life!" the gunfighter snarled. "Shaddrock fucked your woman, lost a Gatling gun and didn't bring back any payment for it. He got three of your men killed in the process and then he badmouths you in front of the rest of us and you stick up for him!"

"I have already explained about Marie," Larson commented. "And Shaddrock is right. The blame for

184

the failure of his mission belongs to me. I shouldn't have trusted that pig Montoya. At least he'll suffer in that *Federale* prison until they hang the *bastardo.*" He shrugged. "Unfortunately, we will now have to move our campsite to the other side of the border."

"But that cavalry patrol damn near blew us to pieces when we made that sale with Black Eagle," Quint reminded him. "We can't set up a headquarters in the United States, for crissake!"

"We can't stay here," Larson insisted. "The *Federales* will be hunting us now and that scum-toad Montoya will tell them everything he knows about where we are. Also, the *rurales* might also be looking for us if anyone at that cantina tells what happened to their commander. The Yankee Army may be more efficient than either the *Federales* or the *rurales,* but the Mexican authorities are far more ruthless and vicious. We move."

"This whole goddamn business is Shaddrock's fault," Quint declared. "What the hell got into you, Ramon?"

"I am the leader of this gang, no?" Larson declared coyly. "So I will decide who is guilty of what—and I will chose my second in command as I see fit."

The pistolman's axe-blade face seemed to harden into granite with two dots of glowing lava for eyes. "What does that mean?"

"Maybe it means a man who thinks fast in a crisis is a better leader than one who is only quick with his *pistola,*" the Comanchero chief answered flatly.

"Is that a fact?" Quint rasped, glaring at Shaddrock.

185

"Ohhh shit," the bounty hunter moaned softly.

"You figure his big mouth is more important than my ability with a six-gun, Ramon?" the pistolman snapped.

"Actually, I think there's room in this outfit for his gun and my mouth," Shaddrock said with a forced grin.

"No there ain't," Quint stated, his voice as cold as frozen coffin nails.

"We'll discuss this later, Quint," Larson told him.

"There ain't nothing to discuss," the gunfighter declared, stepping in front of Shaddrock. "We didn't have no problems with who was second in command until you showed up, feller!"

"Hell." Shaddrock shrugged. "I'm not ambitious. I'll take third in command. Fourth or fifth even."

"You seemed to know which end of a gun does what when you plugged Arlon Ford a while back." Quint smiled thinly. "Let's see how you do against me."

"Quint!" Larson shouted.

"This is between the dude and me," the gunman told him, his gaze still locked on Shaddrock. "I'm waitin' on you, big mouth."

The Comancheros backed away from Quint and the bounty hunter, giving ample room for their deadly contest. Shaddrock sighed and removed his sombrero.

"Don't," Cougar warned in a tense whisper.

"I don't see that he's giving me any choice," Shaddrock replied, tossing the hat aside.

Reluctantly, the senior bounty hunter moved away from his partner, leaving Shaddrock alone to face

Wesley Quint. The younger regulator tried not to think about the pistolman's well-earned reputation. He tried to forget how Quint had drawn and fired two bullets into a man with a gun already in his fist. He failed.

"Whenever you're ready, city slicker," the gunfighter invited.

Shaddrock slipped the poncho over his head and let it fall to the ground. The walnut grips of the twin Police Colts jutted from the now visible shoulder holsters. He extended his left arm and slowly raised it.

"You got it," the bounty hunter replied flatly, his right hand moving to the pistol under his arm.

"You better borrow a hip holster." Quint smiled.

"You better hope somebody can spell your name correctly," Shaddrock replied with a mocking grin. "For the headstone."

Quint's smile vanished. His ugly mouth formed a hard determined line as he stood straddle-legged, hand poised above the butt of his low slung Smith & Wesson. Shaddrock slid one foot back, turning sideways to prevent a smaller target, his left arm held high, his splayed fingers near the grips of his Colt.

Enrique, the camp cook, watched with fascination while he stuffed an entire taco into his mouth and methodically chewed it. Jethro Mackall toyed with the bullwhip slung over his shoulders, his gaze blank as he watched the two combatants. Marie shook her head sadly. Luis cracked his knuckles impatiently. Ramon Larson put a cheroot in his mouth and struck a match.

Cougar's expression remained impassive, but his

187

hand dropped to the Colt Dragoon on his hip. If his partner died, Quint wouldn't live to boast about his accomplishment.

The pistolman's eyes narrowed, his fingers twitched slightly, prepared to draw. Shaddrock still grinned at his opponent as he raised his eyebrows as if inviting Quint to make the first move.

Metal scraped leather and the gunfighter's Smith & Wesson appeared in his hand, hammer cocked and finger on the trigger. Shaddrock's right arm swung forward so fast no one even saw a blur of movement. Orange flame spat from the muzzles of the Police Colt and the Smith & Wesson.

Wesley Quint's body jerked sharply even as he pulled the trigger, causing his aim to weave. The .4 caliber projectile spun past Shaddrock's cheek, nearly searing flesh. The bounty hunter scarcely noticed it as he felt the welcome recoil of the Police Colt ride through his wrist and forearm. Quint staggered backward, mouth open in surprise and pain. Blood stained the left side of his vest.

Shaddrock's pistol roared again. A .36 lead ball hit the gunfighter in the center of the chest, blasting his sternum apart and knocking him to one knee. Quint groaned as his head bobbed weakly and scarlet trickled from his lips. He turned his hatchet face toward Shaddrock and feebly raised his revolver. The bounty hunter's Colt barked a third time. A crimson glob exploded between Wesley Quint's eyes, and the back of his skull vomited splattered brains and blood. The fabled pistolman sprawled on the ground, his lifeless body quivering before muscles and nerves surren dered to death.

"Cristo!" Larson exclaimed as the flame of the match burned to his fingers.

Other onlookers expressed their awe. Enrique coughed loudly, nearly choking on his taco. Marie stared slack-jawed with amazement. Jethro shook his head with disbelief. Juan Alverez gazed down at Quint's corpse as though he expected it to rise at any moment. Cougar sighed with relief.

Shaddrock's hand shook, making it difficult to holster his revolver.

"Quint was so very fast," Alverez muttered dully. "I did not think it was possible . . ."

"Neither did he," Shaddrock remarked, trying to control the nervous reactions that followed a near encounter with violent death. "That's why he's dead."

"Well," Larson mused, lighting his cheroot with another match. "I guess we know who's second in command now, eh? Unless you have some objection, Juan?"

"Oh, no!" the former *bandido* assured his boss—and Shaddrock—his head swinging from side to side vigorously. "I have no complaints, Ramon."

"Bueno," the Comanchero leader declared. "Now that we are once again a large and contented family, it's time to fold up our tents and find a new home."

The gang uttered various groans and sighs at the thought of the task before them, but they shuffled away to obey Larson's orders. Comancheros stepped over and around the corpse of Wesley Quint, already regarding the once feared gunfighter as just a lump of dead meat. Cougar stepped close to Shaddrock.

189

"You all right?" he asked softly.

"I can hardly believe I beat that bastard," Shaddrock confessed in a stunned voice.

"You did." Cougar smiled thinly. "Looks like Larson's going to give us a little help with our mission. At least we'll have him and the Gatling guns on American soil. That takes care of one of our problems."

"The Comancheros have lost about ten men recently," the younger bounty hunter remarked. "But that still leaves about thirty-five or forty men to deal with. What do we do about that?"

"Well." Cougar shrugged. "That's our *other* problem."

SIXTEEN

The Comancheros crossed the border into Texas by dusk. Larson selected a quiet forest area along the Rio Grande for their new campsite. They spent most of the night erecting tents and detailing work to each member of the gang. Shaddrock was put in charge of security. The woods lacked the natural protection of the rock walls the Comancheros utilized at their former site. The bounty hunter posted four guards—east, west, north, and south of the bivouac area. He warned the sentries that if they were found sleeping or intoxicated on duty, he'd personally see to their punishment.

Cougar checked the remaining five Gatling guns and helped Shaddrock select the best positions for the two that would guard the campsite. Two other Gatlings were kept in reserve within the camp. Larson instructed the bounty hunter to leave the last weapon empty but to "polish it up so it looks pretty."

"Sounds like you got another sale set up," Cougar mused, taking a flask of whiskey from his pocket.

"Sí." The outlaw leader nodded, listening to the rippling music of the nearby river. "While you and Shaddrock were frolicking with the Federales, I sent Alverez to pay a visit to another acquaintance of mine."

"An 'old friend' like Tomas Montoya?"

"One of my better customers, like Black Eagle the Kiowa war chief. Perhaps you've heard of him. Stanley Whitman?"

Cougar recognized the name immediately, but he kept his reaction from altering his expression. "Ain't he some sort of outlaw?"

"*Si.*" Larson laughed. "He has made a career of robbing banks and stagecoaches. Trains he leaves to the James and Younger boys. Whitman is either too lazy to try them or he thinks they're too difficult. I wish I could have seen his face when Juan told him about the train robbery *I* masterminded. Of course, he hasn't done too badly either. A bounty hunter could earn two thousand dollars by collecting the price on Stan Whitman's head."

The lengendary Cougar smiled. "Maybe we're in the wrong business, Ramon."

Larson laughed again. "I don't think so, *amigo*. It is safer to sell guns than to try to make a living by going up against men that use them as well as Whitman and his gang."

"Guess it would be pretty risky," the regulator agreed. "But doing business with fellers like that can be too. We got a good example of that recently."

"I know," the Comanchero admitted. "I thought I could trust Tomas, but I should have realized I can't trust anyone. You, Shaddrock, Alverez, Marie— anyone, except myself."

"You plan to go along with us?"

"No. I'm putting Shaddrock in charge of the exchange. Alverez will be there to keep an eye on him and vice versa."

"Who's gonna keep an eye on Whitman?"

"You are, of course," the gang leader replied. "An eye that will be staring through the sights of the other Gatling gun. From now on we handle all exchanges as we did with Black Eagle. Our buyers will purchase a Gatling from us while another gun keeps them covered."

"That's a pretty convincing sales tactic."

Larson smiled. "We're going to get seven hundred dollars from Whitman. He wants a Gatling to reinforce his hideout. It seems he isn't afraid of lawmen, bounty hunters, or the cavalry, but the Texas Rangers scare him shitless. He lives in constant fear that one day the Rangers will come swooping down on him."

"If I were him, I'd be more worried about bounty hunters."

"Oh?" Larson raised an eyebrow. "Why?"

"Texas Rangers have only one reason to want Whitman." Cougar grinned. "A bounty hunter has two thousand."

Because their new locale lacked the stony protection of their old site and the surrounding trees increased the possibility of enemies creeping into the camp, the Comancheros didn't indulge in their customary orgy of tequila, chili, and *putas*. The bivouac area was silent except for the snores that managed to escape from tents and the occasional unhappy mutters of a sentry as he wondered why fate had been cruel enough to give him guard duty while others slept.

Cougar waited until his turnip-shaped watch informed him it was after midnight before he left his cot and stealthily crept from the tent he'd been assigned to. He was surprised to find the object of his quest—Shaddrock—seated on an orange crate by the campfire. The younger bounty hunter held a blue tin cup in both hands. No steam rose from the black liquid in it. Even from behind, Cougar knew his partner was brooding. Shaddrock's whole body seemed to sag when he felt depressed.

"You shouldn't drink that stuff now," the senior bounty hunter remarked, sitting on a nail keg beside his friend. "It'll keep you up. You ought'a get some sleep."

"Yeah," Shaddrock replied dully. The yellow light of the flames displayed his frown and the sadness in his eyes.

Brooding up a storm, Cougar thought. "We got a big day tomorrow. Didn't Larson tell you?"

"He told me." The other man shrugged.

"You know, we lost two of the Gatlings, but if we can manage to get our hands on Stan Whitman that'll more than make up for it. Hell, last I'd heard he was holed up somewhere in the Oklahoma badlands. He should'a stayed there, huh?"

"I guess so," Shaddrock sighed.

"All right." Cougar rolled his eyes with frustration. "What's got you all deflated inside like a homely spinster watching her younger sister gettin' married?"

"Nothing . . ."

"Don't give me that bullshit."

194

"Well." Shaddrock turned to his partner. "I was just thinking about Marie."

Cougar shook his head. "I should have known it had to be a woman on your mind—like usual."

"You saw what Larson did to her," the younger man hissed, fire burning behind his blue orbs more fiercely than the blaze before them. "The son of a bitch tossed her over to that tent of whores so every filthy pig in this camp can mount her like an animal in heat."

"Now don't get upset," his partner began. "But you are aware that she didn't become Larson's mistress after he kidnapped her from a convent."

"So she used to be a high-priced prostitute a while back," Shaddrock allowed. "She told me why she had to leave New Orleans. A fella tried to beat her to death and she shot him."

"Hell," Cougar groaned. "She was stealin' his wallet."

"You figure that gave him a right to kill her?"

"It sure gave him a right to be unhappy with her."

"Cougar . . ."

"All right," the senior hunter sighed. "I don't blame the girl for shooting a feller who was trying to punch her head off, but that still don't make her an angel."

"What if she isn't?" Shaddrock demanded. "Marie still doesn't deserve what Larson's done to her."

"Look, Shaddrock," Cougar began in a weary voice. "Right now there ain't a thing we can do for your damsel in distress. We've got a job to take care of and we've gotta concentrate on keeping *ourselves* alive in order to collect that nice fat reward."

"I won't just leave her here," the younger man declared stubbornly. "I mean it."

"There's nothing you can do tonight except get some rest. We're going to have to be ready for tomorrow. With a little luck, this might be the break we've been waiting for."

"You're probably right," Shaddrock allowed, raising the cup to his lips. He grimaced. "Besides, cold coffee is lousy."

Cougar grinned and placed a hand on his friend's shoulder. "We'll do what we can for the girl," he promised. "You just look after yourself tomorrow. I'll probably be too busy to do it for you."

The following morning, Shaddrock, Cougar, Alverez, and four other Comancheros rode from the campsite. Juan Alverez drove the Conestoga while another ex-*bandido* sat beside him with an L.C. Smith shotgun in his lap. The senior bounty hunter rode in the back of the wagon with the two Gatling guns. Shaddrock and the other three Comancheros escorted the Conestoga on horseback, positioned on both sides of the vehicle.

The little caravan traveled for five hours, moving from the pleasant woods by the Rio Grande to the formidable dry prairies. The area was barren except for sagebrush and irregular rock formations.

"Where the hell is this Whitman character?" Shaddrock asked Alverez, steering his Morgan close to the wagon.

"I know the way, *señor,*" the Mexican outlaw answered. "It is only another mile or so. Be patient."

"I'll be patient until the territory starts looking like

196

Oklahoma," the bounty hunter replied dryly. "Then I'll figure you got us lost."

"Whitman said he would meet us at a waterhole beyond these rocks," Alverez explained, gesturing at the natural sculptures of stone that surrounded them. "It won't be much further."

"I hope not," the regulator sighed. The Texas sun was getting the better of the Easterner's disposition. Although he felt better clad in blue denim, a white Stetson, and a black vest that concealed his shoulder holster rig than he had dressed in Mexican clothing. A ring of sweat already stained the hat. He worried that the moisture under his arms might dampen the powder charges of his cap and ball revolvers.

The sinister click-clack of a lever action carbine startled the group. They turned to see two dust-coated figures in ill-treated cowboy garb positioned by a rock formation at the rear of the Comancheros. More men emerged from other stone monoliths, most of them holding weapons. The amused expressions of the "ambushers" served to ease some of the travelers' concern.

"You boys are right fortunate we was expectin' you," a broad-shouldered man announced, stepping toward the Comancheros. "Otherwise, we would've guessed you was a bunch of greenhorns that got lost with that big ol' wagon o' yore's."

"It's pretty lucky for *you*," Shaddrock replied with a smile. "You fellas wouldn't really want to get your asses shot off by a Gatling because you decided to rob the wrong folks, would you?"

Stan Whitman's frown was almost undetectable

197

amid a great walrus mustache. The brim of his ten-gallon hat covered most of his upper face. As he approached, the outlaw's left hand rested on the grips of a Griswald & Gunnison .36 caliber revolver in a belly holster.

"You must be in charge of this little party, eh?" Whitman inquired.

"That's right," Shaddrock confirmed. He casually counted the men in Whitman's gang: seven less-than-magnificent specimens of Western brutality and meanness. "You fellers just enjoy surprising folks or do you have a reason for popping up here instead of where you said we'd have this meeting?"

"Seein' as how there's a two thousand dollar reward for me now," Whitman answered, "it pays to be sort'a careful."

"Do we look like lousy bounty hunters to you?" Shaddrock demanded.

"You don't exactly look like the sort Ramon Larson usually teams up with neither." The outlaw shrugged. "I'm surprised he didn't send Wesley Quint for a job like this."

"Why would he send a corpse to do a man's job?"

Whitman cocked back the brim of his hat and stared at Shaddrock. "Quint finally meet up with somebody faster than him?"

The regulator nodded. "You're looking at him, fella."

"I'll be damned," the outlaw whispered.

"Guess you'd know more about that than we would," Shaddrock replied. "But before you go to hell, you can pay us for the Gatling we hauled

198

out here."

"Well. . ." Whitman stammered, still stunned that the young Easterner had taken the famous Wesley Quint. "Sure thing."

The Comancheros dragged the first multibarreled death machine from the wagon. They rolled the gun to the outlaws. A column of yellow and brown teeth peeked under Whitman's mustache as he smiled. He examined the weapon while his men drew closer to do likewise. Shaddrock noted with satisfaction that the entire gang was now positioned in front of the wagon.

"Ugly lookin' critter," one of the hootowls remarked, staring down at the Gatling.

"Maybe." Whitman grinned. "But it'll be beautiful to see them Texas Rangers a' droppin' like turds from a horse if'n they ever find our hideout." He glanced up at Shaddrock. "Hey, this thing ain't loaded!"

"That's right," the bounty hunter said. "But that one *is.*"

While the outlaws inspected the gun, Cougar and two Comancheros had hauled out the other Gatling. Whitman and his men looked directly into the muzzles of the second weapon. Cougar crouched behind the gun, hand poised by the crank-operated trigger.

"What the hell are you boys doing?" the outlaw boss asked, his anger flavored with fear.

"Just a little insurance that you don't try to take the merchandise before you pay for it, *señor* Whitman," Alverez explained.

"I'll give you your fuckin' money when I'm sure this here gun is reliable," Whitman snapped.

"Hector, Lazoro," Alverez shouted to his men.

199

"Bring the ammunition."

"Wait a minute," the outlaw leader growled. "I ain't never handled no Gatling gun. Never even seen one up close before. One of you boys show me how it works, damn it."

Still seated on his Morgan, Shaddrock leaned on the saddle horn and smiled. "Our client wants a demonstration, Mr. Crowly."

"So let's give Whitman a sampler," Cougar replied with a shrug.

Then he opened fire with the Gatling gun.

Stanley Albert Whitman's mouth fell open and his eyes bulged in astonishment and terror as he watched fire spit from the revolving muzzles of the weapon pointed at him and his gang. He died with an expression of total shock frozen on his face and five .44 caliber slugs in his chest. Two of his followers joined him in the mysterious universe of death as bullets smashed into them and sent their lifeless bodies to the ground in an eight-limbed pile of convulsing flesh.

An outlaw raised his Henry carbine to his shoulder a fragment of a second before half a dozen rounds propelled his bloodied corpse backward to collide with the nearest rock formation. Another clawed at a holstered sidearm, but a trio of bullets ripped his forearm and elbow into mangled red meat. The force of the multiple gunshots spun the outlaw about and he received four more slugs in the upper back. His spinal column severed, the man fell belly first across the frame of the unloaded Gatling the Whitman gang had planned to purchase.

"Cristo!" Alverez exclaimed, dropping the reins of

the horse team hitched to the Conestoga. He rose from his seat and dragged his pistol from its leather. "Crowly has gone loco!"

His back was turned to Shaddrock, thus he didn't see the bounty hunter draw a Police Colt and almost casually point it at his head. Juan Alverez didn't hear the shot. He barely felt the .36 caliber lead ball that splintered the back of his skull, burned through his brain, and blew his right eyeball out of its socket. The ex-*bandido's* life ended faster than one can say *"mierda"*.

Cougar's unexpected massacre of the Whitman gang had stunned the Comancheros, but Shaddrock's actions were twice as alarming. Their new second in command and the man who'd saved Ramon Larson's life had suddenly shot down one of his own men! Violent men in a ruthless profession, the Comancheros recovered quickly from the shock and turned their weapons toward Shaddrock.

But the bounty hunter was faster.

His left hand had drawn the other Police Colt at the same instant his right-hand pistol blew Alverez's brains into bloodied mush. The second Colt swung to the startled face of a Comanchero on foot. The man lost that face a shred of a second later when a .36 lead ball shattered it.

The revolver in Shaddrock's right fist barked even as he kicked his feet from the stirrups and swung a leg over the rump of his horse. The bullet broke the collarbone of another Comanchero, jolting the victim backward. Shaddrock's other gun then placed a round under the man's jawbone. The slug sizzled through flesh, tongue, and the roof of the Comanchero's mouth to find a home in his brain.

The bounty hunter landed nimbly on his feet. One of Larson's henchmen still on horseback, galloped toward him, reins held in clenched teeth as both hands worked the lever of a Spencer carbine. Shaddrock raised his arms, crossed his wrists and cocked both Colts. The twin pistols erupted. Two bullets struck the rider in the chest, pulverizing his heart and right lung. The impact kicked the Comanchero out of the saddle to topple gracelessly—and lifelessly—to the ground.

Raul Vazquez, the man assigned to ride shotgun on the Conestoga didn't know what to do. When the *gringo* known as Crowly began shooting the Whitman gang, Vazquez prepared to blast the crazy *anglo* with his L.C. Smith twelve gauge. Then the other *Americano* started to kill Comancheros! *Madre de Dios!* Juan's body had literally fallen into Raul's lap! He decided to shoot Shaddrock first, but the blond *bastardo* moved like *relampago,* and *pistolas* blazing death in all directions.

The Gatling gun still roared as the last two members of Whitman's gang staggered and fell, their shirts tattered by bloody bullet holes. Vazquez thought Crowly would be too busy to notice him. He raised his shotgun, but then realized Shaddrock's Colts were now silent. The slow-witted Mexican turned sharply and saw the muzzle of a revolver canted around the edge of the driver's seat.

Flame burst from the barrel of the Police Colt. A very hard, very fast projectile tore into the former bandit's thick belly. He cursed and groaned simultaneously, his body convulsing on the seat. His finger jerked a trigger of the L.C. Smith and exploded a charge of buckshot into the sky. Although trained to overcome gunshyness, the shotgun blast proved too much for the team of horses attached to the Conestoga. The animals burst into a panicked gallop, taking the wagon and the wounded Raul Vazquez with them.

"We'd better catch up with that thing," Cougar stated, jogging over to his partner. "It's got the rest of the ammunition for the Gatlings on it and we'll need the rig to take the guns back to Fort McCullen."

"But first we have to give Ramon Larson our official resignation from the Comancheros," Shaddrock remarked as he opened the cylinder of a Police Colt to reload.

"Yeah," the senior bounty hunter agreed. "And our membership ain't all that'll get terminated before the night's over."

SEVENTEEN

Ezequiel Morales wondered if it was possible for him to go to heaven when he died. The young Comanchero didn't generally contemplate his own mortality or the prospects of his soul's destination after death. However, on quiet nights, when he was alone and sober (which didn't happen often), Morales' thoughts drifted to such matters. That night, as he stood guard duty by one of the Gatling guns positioned to defend the campsite, he recalled his past and fearfully considered the high probability that he'd spend the next life in hell with *El Diablo's* pitchfork up his *nalga*.

Not that Ezequiel thought of himself as evil. True, he was a sinner—more than most, perhaps—but sinners can still find salvation. He'd burned villages, robbed scores of *peones* and small farmers, raped women while they begged for mercy, and he'd shot old men with their hands tied behind their backs—but he had always done these things as part of a group, thus the responsibility for his actions must be shared with others, no? The Lord forgives those that repent and Morales had done so on many occasions. He must have repented a dozen times over the years. Still, he decided he'd better do it again.

"Oh, Father in Heaven," he began, gazing up at the

round pitted face of the full moon that shone between the branches of the surrounding trees. "I'm sorry for all the bad things I've done and all the bad things I'll do in the future."

He nodded with satisfaction. That ought to take care of his soul for a while.

"Who the hell are you talking to?" a voice demanded in English.

With a start, Morales pivoted, his hand dropping to the .44 Army Colt on his hip. To his relief, he saw the two *gringos,* Shaddrock and Crowly, emerge from the shadows.

"Oh, I was singing to myself to stay awake," he replied in broken English. His *machismo* prevented him from admitting he'd been asking God for forgiveness and if he said he'd been talking to himself they might think he was loco.

"Great," Shaddrock said sourly. "That must be why you didn't hear us coming. You're lucky we aren't cavalry troops or Apaches."

"Si," Morales said. He didn't like to think about those *Indio* devils. "How did the sale go?"

"What do you think happened?" Cougar inquired dryly. "Everybody got killed but me and Shaddrock."

The Comanchero smiled weakly, although he didn't find the *gringo's* joke very funny.

"Well," Shaddrock said, stepping closer. "You're being relieved of guard duty."

His brass knuckle-clad fist rose swiftly and caught the unprepared Comanchero under the jaw. Ezequiel Morales' teeth slammed together forcibly and his consciousness evaporated like an icicle in the desert. The

205

young Mexican fell to the ground, arms splayed at his sides. Cougar strolled over and trampled Morales' throat to make certain he never awoke.

"Amen," the bounty hunter rasped.

"What?" his partner asked.

"Before we showed ourselves, he was asking God to forgive him for being a bad boy," Cougar explained.

"Did he do a good job?" Shaddrock inquired. "It was his last chance."

"I ain't much of a prayer critic," the older man replied. "Reckon that's up to God."

"It wouldn't hurt us to say a prayer or two," the other regulator mused.

"You mean you ain't started yet?"

"Ever since we accepted this crazy assignment," Shaddrock admitted.

"Well, our choirboy here was the last sentry." Cougar glanced down at Morales' corpse. "Time to start the main event."

"I hope the curtain only falls on Larson and his men," the younger regulator muttered.

"Just make sure you and me are the only two left alive to take bows," Cougar said.

"Not quite," the younger man declared.

"All right," the senior hunter sighed. "Go get her."

"Don't start the show without me," Shaddrock urged as he turned to leave.

Wishing he'd acquired his partner's catlike (or Cougarlike) ability to move stealthily in the dark, Shaddrock walked to the center of the bivouac area. Every leaf that rustled or twig that snapped under foot sounded like a pistol shot to the bounty hunter. If he encountered a fully awake and sober Comanchero who asked what had happened to the rest of the detail, he hoped he could deal with the man silently. Although he found comfort from the Henry carbine in his grasp, one shot would have the whole gang on him like a pack of gun-wielding jackals.

Despite his concern, Shaddrock reached the *puta* tent unobserved. He knelt by the canvas entrance and softly called Marie's name. A stout, fat-faced woman with greasy black hair emerged instead.

"Marie is not feeling too well, *señor,*" the whore remarked smugly. "But Josefia is in the mood for love." She smiled, revealing the few tobacco stained teeth she still retained.

"Some other time," Shaddrock replied, trying to hold his breath and talk at the same time. The woman's body odor could make a skunk puke. "I have to talk to Marie."

"She don't want to be disturbed." Josefia pouted.

"Alex?" a female within the tent asked weakly. "That you?"

"Marie?" the bounty hunter inquired. The voice hadn't sounded like the redhead's.

When Marie emerged from the tent, he saw why. Both her lips were split. Dried blood caked her cut mouth and nostrils. The girl's cheeks had been viciously scratched, leaving angry red trails on both sides of her face. Marie's left eye was swollen shut and surrounded by an ugly purple bruise.

"Jesus," Shaddrock whispered.

"Seems the other girls sort'a resented me," Marie

said, speaking thickly through torn lips.

He held the carbine in one fist to embrace Marie with a free arm. "It'll be all right," the bounty hunter told her gently.

"She's not so pretty now, eh?" Josefia laughed, putting her hands on her wide hips. "Maybe you ready to fuck with me now, no? Josefia don't have any ugly marks on her face."

"Wanta bet?" Shaddrock growled.

He released Marie and raised the Henry in both fists, punting the brass frame into the whore's grinning mouth with all the strength his arms could muster. Josefia's head snapped back, tentacles of oily hair flying. Then she crashed to the ground like an overweight tree. Marie gasped.

"Cougar and I might have tried to spare the other girls," the bounty hunter hissed. "But not now. The bitches deserve what they're going to get."

"What are you talking about, Alex?" Marie asked, stunned by his actions and confused by his words.

"We're leaving this place, hon," Shaddrock replied.

"Are you crazy? Ramon'll never let us go . . ."

"Ramon's coming with us," the regulator smiled. "All ten thousand dollars of him."

Shaddrock and Marie moved to a Gatling gun stationed at the east side of the camp. Its multiple barrels had already been directed toward the center of the bivouac area. The bounty hunter handed the girl his carbine.

"Use it if you have to," he instructed, kneeling behind the Gatling gun.

"What are you doing?" Marie asked in a dazed tone. Then the obvious implications of his actions struck home. "Oh, shit!"

"We're going to blast the Comancheros to hell," Shaddrock announced.

"That's crazy!" she exclaimed. "There's almost fifty guys down there and they're all meaner than a pissed off rattler!"

"Pretty soon they'll all be deader than a rusty coffin nail."

"You can't get them all by yourself—even with this thing." Marie thrust a finger at the Gatling.

"I'm not all by myself."

"You aren't counting on me, are you?" she glared at him with her good eye. "Do you think I'm a female Davy Crockett? I never fired one of these repeaters before."

"So?" Shaddrock grinned. "This'll be my first time with a Gatling gun too. But a real expert told me how to handle it." The regulator pointed to the west. "And there he is."

Cougar's head rose above some bushes on the opposite side of the camp as he watched the couple get ready.

"Crowly's in on this with you?" Marie's mouth opened in awe. "How'd you talk him into this?"

"We've been working together for over a year, hon," he replied. "That's my partner—Thomas Cruthers, better known as Cougar."

"Your partner?" she shook her head. "Who are you? What are you?"

"Half of the team of Shaddrock and Cougar," he an-

209

swered proudly. "The best bounty hunters in the West. And we're about to prove it and earn twenty thousand bucks in the process."

The senior bounty hunter sighed. "Come on, Shaddrock," he whispered through clenched teeth. "Yak with the girl later. We got some killing to do."

Finally, his partner held up a thumb to indicate he was ready.

"Glad you could spare the time." Cougar rolled his eyes with exasperation.

The veteran man hunter walked to his Gatling gun and sat on an apple crate behind it. He placed his hand on the crank-trigger and took a deep breath.

"Time to start the fireworks," he rasped.

The metallic chatter of the rapid-fire weapon ripped into the night like a telegraph key in the hands of a giant maniac. Pure hell in the form of lead projectiles rained down on the Comanchero camp. Bullet holes appeared in canvas and tents deflated into twitching lumps of canvas as wounded men staggered into tent poles. Men emerged from other sections of the camp, pistols and long guns in hand. Shaddrock's Gatling joined in the *rat-tat-tat* song of death. Forty-four caliber slugs slammed into the Comancheros, hurtling their screaming bodies to the ground.

"Look at those sons of bitches drop," Shaddrock said, awestruck by the destruction he was creating.

"There's still plenty more that are on their feet," Marie warned.

Enrique, the camp cook, ran for the cover of the treeline to the north of the bivouac area. Cougar tracked the obese Mexican with his Gatling and gave

he crank an almost delicate turn. Three rounds
punched into Enrique's fat torso. The cook cried out
as he sprawled on his face.

Four terrified and totally naked whores burst from
the *puta* tent, utterly panicstricken by the carnage.
One tripped over the unconscious figure of Josefia.
Marie smiled coldly as she raised the Henry to her
shoulder and squeezed off a shot. A whore screamed
when the .44-40 slug ripped through her flabby right
breast and tunneled into the equally fleshy left before
entering her heart.

Marie worked the lever of the carbine and blasted
another naked harlot in the lower back, the bullet
striking two inches above the woman's quivering fat
rump. The base of her spine exploded in white agony
and the slut crashed to the earth with a terrible
shriek. Shaddrock contributed a burst of rapid-fire
fury, pitching the remaining prostitutes into the here-
after. Josefia recovered her senses. With both upper
and lower jaws broken, she couldn't even scream
when the Gatling slugs punctured her flesh.

"I hope those demons in hell have spikes on their
peckers and molten lead for sperm," Marie hissed.

Shaddrock failed to hear her remark as he turned
the Gatling on Ramon Larson's tent. Bullets peppered canvas, but the bounty hunter couldn't tell
whether or not any rounds found their intended target. A sudden volley of lead spat dirt in front of the
bounty hunter and pelted trees surrounding his position.

"They're using the Gatling they kept in reserve inside the camp!" Marie exclaimed.

"No shit?" Shaddrock snorted.

Three Comancheros had rolled the rapid-fire weapon from its hiding place inside one of the tents and directed its fire at the regulator's site. Shaddrock and Marie threw themselves to the ground as the deadly barrage burned air above them. The pair remained pinned down until Cougar's Gatling came to the rescue.

A quick burst of .44 slugs tore into two of the Comanchero gunners. The men flew from their weapon, bodies rolling like bloodied tumbleweeds. The survivor of the trio desperately shifted the Gatling toward Cougar's position and knelt behind it.

Seizing advantage of the distraction, Shaddrock rose and quickly cranked his gun, sending a salvo of lead into the enemy Gatling gunner. Bullets blasted the Comanchero's skull into crimson paste. Other rounds struck the frame of the weapon. Cartridges burst within the chambers. The rear of the Gatling seemed to explode like a giant firecracker.

"Damn it, Shaddrock!" Cougar's voice called out. "Don't fuck up any of the Gatling guns!"

"What the hell was I supposed to do?" the younger bounty hunter shouted back.

Before Cougar could respond, a group of Comancheros opened fire in his direction with rifles and carbines. A bullet ricocheted off one of the Gatling' barrels. Another hissed past the bounty hunter's ear, tugging at the wide brim of his Montana peak hat. The grizzled veteran of violent encounters barely flinched. Cougar shifted the Gatling and fired down on the marksmen. Shaddrock followed his example.

Almost fifty rounds smashed into the Comancheros like a tidal wave of death. The men screamed, their bodies hopping and jerking like drunken Indians before they crumpled to the ground. The shooting stopped abruptly. The only sounds were the ringing inside the ears of the living participants of the battle and their own exhilarated heart beats.

"Hey, Cougar!" Shaddrock yelled. "This thing's out of amunition. How the hell do you reload it?"

"Figure it out for yourself!" his partner shouted in reply as he tried to cope with his weapon which had jammed. "I got my own problems!"

"Asshole!" the younger regulator snapped. "Guess it doesn't matter anyway. I think we got 'em all!"

"Better make damn sure of it!" Cougar told him, wishing he had a knife to pry a mishapen cartridge case from the breech of the gun. With a sigh, he gathered up his shotgun and abandoned the Gatling.

"Stay here," Shaddrock told Marie, drawing his Police Colts from their holsters.

"Where are you going?" she demanded.

"Everybody down there is supposed to be dead," he replied. "I just want to make sure they *know* it."

Pedro Gonzales cursed the two *gringos* he'd praised so highly the day before. *Cristo!* How could they have fooled him so completely? Of course, Shaddrock and Crowly (if that's who they really were) had tricked Ramon Larson and the others as well. Limping painfully from a Gatling bullet in his left thigh, Pedro and Amado Gomara, another Comanchero, laboriously moved through the forest beyond the perimeter of the camp.

"You think all the others are dead, Pedro?" Amado asked, a quiver of fear accenting his voice. He held a Whitney Colt in his right hand while his left clutched a deep bullet crease in his side.

"Those anglo *bastardos* are still alive," Gonzales snapped. "But they won't be much longer."

"They're dangerous *hombres,*" Amado whined.

"But their Gatling guns no longer roar." Pedro smiled. "If we circle around behind them, one at a time, we can blow the *gringos* to hell!"

"Like this?" a voice inquired behind the pair.

The Comancheros whirled, pistols held ready, thumbs earring back hammers with desperate speed. An explosion of orange light accompanied the fierce bellow of Cougar's shotgun. Buckshot tore into Amado Gomara's face and throat. The featureless corpse hadn't completed its fall to earth before the Greener's other barrel erupted. Pedro Gonzales managed to scream as the multiple pellets transformed his chest into strawberry-colored gore.

The bounty hunter remained in the shadows and prepared to break open his shotgun to reload. Suddenly, two large hands seized the twin barrels and ripped the shotgun from his grasp. The unexpected tug was so forceful, it threw Cougar off balance and he toppled backward. Luis towered over him. The huge Mexican's white teeth seemed to glow in the dim moonlight.

"I told you I'd kill you!" he hissed, raising the shotgun overhead.

Cougar jerked his Colt Dragoon from its holster. A heavy boot stomped on his hand. The regulator

214

groaned as Luis slid his foot to one side and sent the pistol skidding out of its owner's reach. He swung the Greener at his victim's skull like a club.

The bounty hunter pulled his head aside and the walnut stock stamped the ground next to his ear. Cougar rolled onto his shoulders and thrust the bottom of his foot into Luis' grinning face. The Mexican grunted and staggered back two steps. Cougar scrambled to his feet.

Blood trickled from Luis' broken nose as he snarled with rage and swung the shotgun in a vicious backhand sweep. The regulator jumped out of range. The Greener smashed into a tree trunk, its stock splitting on impact. Cougar's hand lashed out, the edge of his semiclosed fist chopping the Mexican's wrist like an axe. The shotgun fell from Luis' numb fingers.

Extremely fast for a man his size, Luis slammed a fist into the bounty hunter's jaw, knocking him into another tree. The breath spewed from Cougar's lungs when his back connected with the trunk. The big Mexican lunged forward, determined to tear his opponent apart with his bare hands.

Dodging swiftly, Cougar avoided the deadly fingers and jabbed a fist under Luis' heart. The Comanchero growled, more annoyed than hurt by the blow. But the bounty hunter moved behind his adversary and hit him with a fast punch to a kidney, followed by a stroke between the shoulder blades with the bottom of his fist. Luis stumbled forward, his forehead striking the tree trunk.

Yet, the Mexican giant whirled and attacked again, oblivious to the blood that streamed from his gashed brow. The regulator's arms rose quickly. Luis reached out, trying to seize one of his foe's arms to pull him closer. Cougar's move was a feint. He suddenly dropped to one knee and drove a vicious punch directly between the Mexican's legs.

A retching gasp was emitted from Luis as his body stiffened with agony. He doubled up, clawing at his crotch. Cougar's fist cracked into the side of the big man's skull. Luis fell to his knees. Swiftly, the bounty hunter hopped to his feet and whipped a back-fist to his opponent's temple. The Mexican fell to all fours with a groan.

Cougar closed in. He straddled Luis like a horse and grabbed his hair with one hand as the other gripped him under the chin. Both men sprawled to the ground. The bounty hunter's legs wrapped around the larger man's chest, pinning his arms. Luis realized what the regulator was about to do. He struggled to break free, but Cougar savagely twisted the Mexican's head. Vertebra snapped with an ugly crunch of grating bone. Luis trembled violently, blood oozing from his ears and mouth. Then his body went limp.

Cougar released the dead man, allowing Luis' head to dangle loosely by its broken neck. The regulator rose weakly and staggered to his discarded Dragoon pistol.

"I reckon we ain't ever gonna be friends, Luis," he muttered.

Shaddrock moved cautiously into the campsite, both Police Colts held ready. The bounty hunters had previously discussed the clean up procedure after bombarding the Comancheros with the Gatling guns. First they'd check the surrounding area and then inspect the camp itself for survivors.

The latter part of the job also offered the highest risk since the ground was literally covered with dead—or apparently dead—Comancheros. Shaddrock heard his partner's shotgun and knew Cougar had encountered two or more opponents at the treeline. He felt concern for his friend, but he shoved it into the back of his mind. Cougar could take care of himself and Shaddrock had to concentrate on his present task.

He examined the corpses one by one, glancing about occasionally in case another "dead man" was waiting for an opportunity to blast the regulator. The result of multiple rapid-fire bullets on human beings had been devastating. Splintered bone protruded from flesh. Faces and skulls were smashed into crimson smears. Blood formed red puddles where concentrated Gatling slugs had slain groups of Comancheros. Shaddrock hadn't seen such destruction since the War between the States.

Something hissed vehemently near the regulator. He pivoted and glimpsed the blur of a long black serpent of leather. Shaddrock tried to dodge the lash, but it was too quick. The whip struck his extended arms, curling around his wrists like the tentacle of a killer squid. Jethro Mackall clenched his teeth as he pulled the bullwhip forcibly. The Police Colts popped out of the bounty hunter's grasp as the sudden tug sent Shaddrock tumbling to the ground.

"Got ye now, bas-turd!" the hillbilly growled,

drawing back his lash. "I's gonna whip yore hide clean off'a ye like it was a corn husk!"

Mackall savagely swung his weapon. The twisted cord struck the regulator's back as he scrambled to all fours, slashing cloth and slicing skin like a knife. Shaddrock groaned and the lash struck again, cutting flesh and bruising muscle. Mackall's arm jerked back and forth wildly, hurling the whip with deadly skill and speed. Blood seeped through Shaddrock's torn shirt as the lash struck again.

Desperately, the bounty hunter rolled across the ground, his teeth grinding together when his injured back met hard earth. The whip hit his chest and exploded another wave of agony when it bit into his pectoral muscles. Shaddrock's hands groped out for the leather tormentor, but the bullwhip was too fast and slippery and wielded by an expert.

"Fuck it," the regulator hissed, dipping a hand into his vest pocket.

Turning on his side, he jerked the derringer free, aimed the diminutive pistol and cocked its hammer. A lash stroke cut into his triceps, jerking his arm as he fired. Mackall cried out, stumbled, and fell.

Gasping for breath, Shaddrock rose to his feet. The empty derringer dropped from his fingers. *The hell with it,* he thought, walking on unsteady legs to his Colt pistols. *I'll get it later.* The regulator bent to retrive his revolvers.

A shadow fell across him. He turned to see the wrathful figure of Jethro Mackall, his bullwhip clenched between clenched fists. Bellowing like a wounded beast, the hillbilly tossed the lash over

Shaddrock's head. The leather loop closed around the regulator's neck. Mackall jerked his fists and tightened the whip like a garrote.

The bounty hunter struggled wildly, driving a knee into the Comanchero's groin. A hissing groan escaped from the red-bearded face inches from Shaddrock's own. A trickle of blood beneath Mackall's left eye revealed where the .36 caliber derringer round had split cheekbone, but failed (due to the size of the projectile and the shortness of the gun barrel) to penetrate.

The constriction increased. Both men fell to the ground. Shaddrock kicked and punched with all his rapidly dwindling strength to strangle him. Mackall believed he would die from the gunshot wound and he intended to take his assassin with him to the grave.

Consciousness and life itself began to slip from Shaddrock. His panic-raked mind retained enough calm to remember the only weapon he still possessed. Reaching into his pants pocket, his hand emerged with the brass knuckle-dusters.

The bounty hunter's free hand caught the hillbilly's dirty red hair and pressed it against the ground. Summoning up every ounce of might left in his oxygen-starved body, Shaddrock slammed the edge of the brass knuckles into his opponent's skull. He hammered metal into the side of Mackall's head. The Comanchero's temple exploded, bone shards entering his brain like tiny arrowheads. Jethro Mackall quivered and convulsed, but death had already robbed his body of its strength.

Shaddrock pried the leather noose from his neck and slowly rose to one knee beside the corpse. He

trembled and coughed as his throat refused to func
tion. The campsite rolled before his eyes as though a
earthquake had begun. Gradually, his head cleare
and he weakly climbed to his feet.

"You don't die easy, Shaddrock," a voice declare
The bounty hunter raised his head and saw Ramo
Larson emerge from the bullet-pitted remnants of hi
tent. The Comanchero leader's handsome dark fac
was streaked with dirt and his white shirt had bloo
stains from a bullet wound in his upper chest. Larso
still wore the cutlass in his sash, but the silverplate
Remington revolver in his hand was aimed at Sha
drock as he thumbed back the hammer.

"Neither do I," Ramon continued. "But I think yo
die first, no?"

EIGHTEEN

The shot echoed within the Comanchero camp, the concussion traveling amid the natural ceiling of tree branches. Shaddrock watched in amazement as Ramon Larson's arm suddenly spun across his chest, blood spitting from a shattered elbow. Larson screamed and the Remington jumped from his hand. The Comanchero pivoted with the momentum and broke into an awkward run, clutching his broken arm with his good hand.

"Alex!" Marie's voice called as she hurried forward, smoke curling from the muzzle of the Henry carbine in her grasp. "Are you all right?"

"Thanks to you," he replied. "Why didn't you kill the bastard?"

"I was trying to," she assured him. "But I'm not very good with this thing."

"You should have put another bullet in him when he started to run."

"What bullets?" Marie snorted. "The carbine is out of ammo and *you* didn't leave any shells."

"Give it here," he instructed, taking the Henry. Shaddrock extracted some cartridges from his belt and fed them into the tubular magazine. "Stay here and wait for Cougar. Use my Colts if you have to—

just make sure you don't shoot Cougar or me."

"You're going after Ramon?"

"Who says there's no such thing as a stupid question," Shaddrock rasped as he jogged from the camp.

The bounty hunter jacked a round into the Henry's chamber as he pursued the Comanchero boss into the treeline. The sound of his quarry thrashing through the bushes told the regulator Larson hadn't gotten far. The outlaw was wounded and losing blood fast. This knowledge charged Shaddrock with eager expectation. He ignored the stiffness and pain of his own injuries and dashed on.

The forest ended by the bank of the Rio Grande. Shaddrock emerged from the trees and skidded to a halt, the carbine held ready. The bounty hunter frowned, considering the possibility his prey may have jumped into the river and swam to the other side. He dismissed the idea because Larson was too badly hurt to attempt such a suicidal method of escape. He had to be somewhere close by...

"Aaaeeeii!"

The scream of rage sent shards of ice up Shaddrock's spine as he whirled to confront the ominous shape that materialized from the shadows. Moonlight reflected on the long curved sliver of steel that swooped down at the bounty hunter's upturned face.

Shaddrock raised the Henry in his fists. The blade of Ramon Larson's cutlass clanged against the brass frame of the carbine. The regulator saw the Comanchero's sweat-coated, terror-filled face an instant before he whipped the wooden stock of his weapon into it. Larson groaned as the butt stroke propelled him backward. He stumbled to the edge of the bank and toppled into the river.

Water splashed Shaddrock's trousers. The bounty hunter stepped closer and watched Ramon Larson struggle weakly in the Rio Grande as the current dragged the semiconscious Comanchero leader downriver. Larson's unbroken arm thrashed hopelessly. His scream sounded as though he was gargling, water filling his mouth and lungs. The man's head disappeared and a still lump continued to travel along the current.

The sun rose higher in the sky as morning approached noon. Cougar frowned as he led his Appaloosa along the bank of the Rio Grande. Shaddrock stared at the water with resentment.

"There ain't any point in going further downriver," the senior bounty hunter remarked. "The current probably hauled Larson's body to the Gulf of Mexico by now."

"He might have lived and managed to drag himself onto the shore . . ."

"Not shot up that way," the older man insisted. "Besides, I looked for evidence in the mud on both sides of the river. If he didn't manage to get out of the water before he got this far, it's because he's dead. He drowned and took a one way trip to the gulf. He's fish food by now."

"Maybe his corpse floated to shore further . . ."

"We lost him, Shaddrock," Cougar sighed.

"Shit!" the younger regulator hissed. "Even dead that son of a bitch had to screw things up!"

"Marie's still waiting for us with a Conestoga full of Gatling guns." Cougar smiled. "We've got five guns. One's a little shot up, but the Army might pay us for it. Even if they don't, we'll also get two thousand for Stan Whitman . . ."

"After everything we went through and then we lose Larson." The other bounty hunter shook his head with dismay.

"We'll still get at least ten thousand," his partner reminded him. "That ain't such a bad bounty."

"Unless you were expecting to get *twenty* thousand," Shaddrock sighed. "Oh, hell. Let's get out of here."